ROSA

WITHDRAWN
FROM STOCK

ROSALIE

CHAPTER ONE

Rosalie Harvey sprang lightly over the fast-running stream in Rayleigh Wood. She jumped with the agility of one used to such habits. Were she not alone, she would have walked further upstream and crossed sedately by the wooden footbridge. Today, Rosalie was in a hurry. She trod carelessly, crushing periwinkles and wood mallow underfoot; pushing past well-laden blackberries with little regard for the elegant gown that she wore. Today, she ignored the grey squirrels who scurried skywards as she passed. She did not smell the damp moss, nor hear the woodpeckers' persistent tapping. Her young face was tense, her blue eyes troubled. She gripped a letter tightly in her hand.

Robert James was out when she was shown into the drawing-room of Rayleigh House. Rosalie was distraught. She had just returned to her home after a dutiful visit to an aunt. The letter she had found explaining the absence of her two young brothers had made her sick with worry. Robert's mother assured her that he would soon be home. Rosalie waited. Self-consciously, she straightened her gown, listening for the sound of hoofbeats on the drive. Why did he take so long? Was that a horse? No—it was just the gardener passing under the window with his wheelbarrow.

Suddenly, impulsively, as if she could bear it no longer, Rosalie handed the letter to Emily James. Robert's mother frowned as she read, her nose wrinkled; she shook her head incredulously. She had always said that Rosalie's young brothers were in need of their dead father's sterner hand. But to run away to sea—well, really! Even she would hardly have expected that of them.

The door burst open. A young man breezed in; dressed in white riding breeches and a black velvet, cut-away coat. His brown hair was taken back in a matching velvet bow. Obviously delighted to see his guest, he came towards her, taking her hand.

'Rosalie. How nice to see you—' He broke off abruptly, seeing her worried face, then frowned. 'Rosalie! Is something wrong? Mother, is something wrong?' he demanded anxiously.

'It's Peter and Ben,' Rosalie explained, her eyes begging him not to be angry.

Robert waved his arms with exasperation. 'What have they been up to now?' he sighed.

His mother handed him the letter. 'They have run away to sea, Robert,' she said with a ring of satisfaction in her voice.

He read it in silence, pacing slowly up and down, one hand behind his back.

'They don't say where they have gone. Do you know, Rosalie? Have they gone to join the Navy?'

She shook her head, her eyes grave with the responsibility left by the death of her father, only a year ago. Her mother had died in childbirth when Ben had been born.

'I don't know, Robert.' She sighed. 'But I have fears that their foolishness might be even greater than we suppose.'

Robert stopped pacing. He stared at her blankly. 'What do you mean?' he said.

'In recent weeks there has been much talk at home of smugglers on the Cornish coast.'

'Smugglers!' Robert's eyes widened with amazement.

'Yes, my father told us many tales of smuggling. I fear the boys considered it a noble thing, sailing from France with the Revenue boats in hot pursuit.'

'You think they may go to Cornwall!' He frowned. 'Most unlikely.'

He sat down abruptly beside her, his face already showing signs of anger. 'Most unlikely,' he repeated curtly. When Rosalie's father had died he had felt an immediate responsibility for the three children. His main concern, however, was for Rosalie; this twenty-year-old girl who was so much a part of his life. He had been glad of the excuse to call on her often, but the boys! They had gone too far now.

He glanced at Rosalie, then seeing her near to tears he took her hand and pressed it firmly.

3

'I suppose we must try to find them,' he said, trying to sound encouraging.

She blinked back the tears in an effort to smile. She came to Robert so often for advice, although he was only four years older than she.

Robert crossed the room to his heavy walnut writing desk and sat down. He took up a quill in his long, lean fingers and tapped it thoughtfully on his chin.

'I'll send to enquire if they left by stage,' he called, beginning to write. 'And letters to London. They may try to join the Navy, even if they have to lie about Ben's age.'

Rosalie felt the tenseness melting away. Shocked, unable to think clearly when she had found the boys gone, she had trusted in Robert's good sense.

'I am really grateful, Robert,' she said. 'I should not have left them. My visit to my aunt was ill timed indeed. They would not have left, had I been here.'

Emily James closed her fan with a flourish. 'Those boys deserve to be whipped,' she said harshly. 'They will find they have chosen badly. A life at sea, so I hear, is not the easy life to which they are accustomed.'

Robert ignored his mother's remarks and went to the door to summon the carriage.

'I'll take you home, Rosalie,' he said, deciding to extricate her immediately from the cynical comments his mother seemed determined to make. 'The boys may think that they were not four-legged. 'The reason I called you, Mr Jennings, is that I need to go away for a time. The length of which I have no way of determining. This would mean that I would leave you entirely responsible for the mill. I take no part in its running. I do, however, have the ultimate right of decision. I will not be available for even this.'

Mr Jennings nodded, feeling somewhat relieved.

'The mill will always continue in the way your father would have wanted it, Mistress Harvey.' He paused, considering. 'However,' he cleared his throat, 'in view of what you have told me, I would like your authority to convert the mill to the mule machine.' He had been weighing up the possibility for some time. 'I fear this is the only way we can hope to regain the good sales we have had in the past,' he added, pressing the point.

Rosalie smiled. 'My father always spoke highly of your judgement, Mr Jennings. I respect it, too. Before I leave I will see you have my consent in writing.'

When the meeting was over, Rosalie felt encouraged, but the hardest part lay ahead. She decided against taking the carriage to Rayleigh. The air and the walk would, she hoped, give her the much-needed courage.

Robert was inspecting his stables with his groom when she arrived. He greeted her with his usual affection. She felt a pang of regret that she was about to incur his disapproval.

'I've something to tell you, Robert,' she said boldly when the groom had been dismissed. 'I'm going to Cornwall to look for the boys.'

Robert threw back his head and laughed heartily. Rosalie felt extremely annoyed.

'Why do you laugh?' she cried angrily. 'I'm in earnest. I am going to Cornwall.'

'And how far will you get alone?' he asked, still laughing.

'If you cannot be serious, Robert, I shall leave and make my own arrangements.' She turned to leave, but he caught her hand and held it, realising he had hurt her.

'Come inside,' he said. 'We'll talk about it.' He led the way into the house and ordered tea. Then he sat down beside her, watching her face as he spoke.

'You must know, Rosalie, that I could never allow you to do such a thing.' He paused, then went on. 'I'm very—fond of you. I could never condone anything that would put you in such danger.'

Rosalie clasped her hands tightly together on her lap. She stared down at the blue carpet. 'I shall go to Cornwall, Robert,' she said. 'Nothing you can say will make me change my mind. My father would have gone, so I must take his place. I came to ask your help.' She looked up at him hopefully. 'I seem to remember you have an acquaintance in North Cornwall. A mine-owner, I believe. Would you give me a letter of introduction that I might ask his advice on accommodation when I arrive?'

Robert's face showed both anger and confusion. His fingers tapped nervously on the arm of the sofa. He said nothing.

Rosalie sighed, then shrugged her shoulders. 'If you do not wish to help me, then no matter. Thank you for sending letters to London. I'll write to you if you wish. If not, then my solicitor will have my address.' She rose from her seat, holding out her hand for him to bid her farewell. He grabbed it firmly, pulling her to him as he stood up.

'Rosalie, I'll not let you go. I intend to marry you. I cannot let my future wife go gallivanting around the countryside.' He was a little shocked at his own vehemence.

She pulled away from him, her head in the air. She walked to the window, where she stood looking out over the lawns. So many memories in these gardens. The places she and Robert had played together as children; talked and laughed as they grew older.

'I was not aware,' she said coolly, 'that I had made any promise of marriage to you, Robert.'

He came towards her, smiling ruefully; he took her hand in his and pressed it to his lips.

'Rosalie—I love you. Marry me. Forget this foolish notion. I'll send a man to Cornwall to search for your brothers.' He waited, less sure of himself now.

She turned her head from the window and

looked up into his warm brown eyes. 'Thank you for the honour of asking me to be your wife, Robert; but I do not feel ready to marry. My search in Cornwall must come first. If I were ready,' she paused, 'then I am sure I would marry you. I have thoughts of no one else.' She pulled her hand quickly out of his, turning her face away. It would take little to cause her to waver.

She could not bear to see the look of hurt pride that would be in his eyes.

He did not follow her as she walked quickly home to Charlesworth Hall. She doubted her own sanity in refusing a man with whom she was so much at ease. Her promise to her father was, however, foremost in her mind. Whatever happened, she must find her brothers; only then could she think of herself.

CHAPTER TWO

Doubts and fears began plaguing Rosalie. The long, wearying journey in the coach had made her body ache, her heart dispirited. She worried about her lack of experience for the task she had set herself. Seeking to forget for a while the incessant tossing, she tried to sleep. The roads became increasingly pitted and rough as they travelled westwards.

The days before her departure had been full,

her mind too busy with arrangements for her absence to allow her to examine thoroughly what she was doing. Even Robert had given up trying to dissuade her. He had visited her just before she left, repeating his offer of marriage. When she had refused again, he had produced a letter from his pocket for Sir Hugh Trevia, tin mine and land owner. He had a large house at Trevia in the parish of Camelford.

'I have requested that you be accepted as a guest in his house,' Robert had explained. She had also found a list of suggestions for her journey. Dear Robert, she thought. He had still helped her, in spite of what must have been a severe blow to his pride.

Enquiries at inns on the way encouraged her to believe that her brothers had certainly travelled ahead of her. As the coachman slowed his horses to descend into the small town of Camelford, she found her doubts vanishing, a feeling of strange excitement replacing them. They were within four miles of the sea; Rosalie had never seen the sea. The prospect of standing close to the ocean of which she had heard and read so much was thrilling her already.

The coach halted briefly at the toll house, then the Cleveland bays clattered over the grey stone bridge, past several Kiddley Winks and inns. The coachman shouted noisily, encouraging them up the narrow hill. The timber houses left barely enough room for the coach to pass. Half-way up the hill, the coach swung acutely left, creaking to a halt in the wide yard of the King's Arms. The smell of pigs filled her nostrils as she climbed down. The hour was late; darkness had fallen as they crossed Davidstow Moor. Heeding Robert's advice, she took a room at the inn for the night. A welcome, still room after days of weary travel.

When morning came, she requested the landlord, Robert Polsue, to send a rider with the letter of introduction to Trevia. Then she waited, alone and apprehensive, for the carriage to arrive. Hugh Trevia was in London when the messenger arrived, but his twenty-five-year-old wife received the letter with pleasure. Lady Lucy Trevia had herself lived in London before her marriage. She found the Cornish countryside gave her little pleasure. The people were rough and uncouth. The prospect of having a guest to stay who was near her own age was decidedly agreeable. She sent the carriage to fetch Rosalie at once.

The granite-walled Trevia House seemed ugly to Rosalie. It was ill designed, seeming to be built haphazardly with little regard for the overall design. The welcome she received was warm; she was relieved to find herself not an unwelcome guest, despite the sense of intrusion that she felt.

'Do you ride?' the auburn-haired Lucy had asked eagerly soon after Rosalie's arrival.

'Indeed I do,' came the quick reply, for Rosalie was delighted to find an excellent stable of horses. She had at first wondered how she would be able to carry out her search without transportation.

The first day at Trevia she needed to recover from the long, tedious journey. But the second day, the thirteenth of September, Rosalie began in earnest. She had woken early, expecting to see autumn sunshine; the view over the valley was blanketed completely by a pale grey mist. She shivered at the dampness. The coal fire in her room was black. She dressed hurriedly and went down for breakfast. It was barely seven o'clock. The servants were astounded. The lady of the house rose late. The maid apologised profusely that she had not lit the fire early enough, vowing that if the mistress was in the habit of rising so early it would be done in future.

After breakfasting, Rosalie enquired, as casually as possible, about smugglers. The maids turned their heads and giggled in corners.

Blueitt, the butler, after clearing his throat several times, suggested that Mistress Harvey would really have to ask Lady Trevia about such things, then excused himself hurriedly.

Rosalie persisted. She went down into the kitchen, ignoring the surprised glances, and asked loudly:

'Is there anyone here who could introduce

me to a smuggler?' The silence that ensued was complete. The cook stopped stirring and stared open-mouthed. No one moved. She might have asked them the way to the moon, by the response she got.

'Have you all lost your tongues?' she cried angrily.

An old man sitting in the corner found his voice. 'Nay, Mistress, we've nay, but no one knows smugglers. Tain't wise.'

Rosalie stamped her foot impatiently. 'I hear,' she said, 'that a large proportion of the population are involved in smuggling, yet you tell me no one knows smugglers.'

The old man spoke again. 'Nay, Mistress. I said tain't wise to know 'ee. Twould bring danger to we, to inform.'

Rosalie sighed. She had not bargained for this. She tapped the floor nervously with her foot, thinking. Still silent, the servants went about their work. Rosalie spoke again, more kindly this time, understanding now that it was fear, not impudence, that prevented their helping.

'I did not mean to put anyone in danger,' she said, not even sure they were listening. She explained her reason for coming to Cornwall. 'So you see,' she went on, 'I must get to know some smugglers.' She looked anxiously around; the response was the same. Faces that said nothing. 'If anyone can help me, perhaps you will tell me when we are alone. I'll pay you well.' She turned to the door, then added as an afterthought, 'I've no wish to judge smuggling, no intention of reporting anyone to the preventive officers. I just wish to find my brothers.' She swept out of the room, smiling a little at the buzz of conversation that arose as soon as she had left.

By the time Lucy Trevia ventured from her room, the mist had lifted a little, but the distant moor was still wrapped in a dark cloud. It was raining heavily. The drive to the house was a sea of well-churned mud, the groom having taken the horses out for exercise, assuming that the ladies would not be riding on such a day.

Lucy was intrigued when Rosalie had explained her mission.

'You'll take me with you if you go out,' she had requested earnestly, longing for a little excitement. 'I so rarely go to London, Rosalie. My husband prefers that I stay in Cornwall.' She omitted to say that she knew only too well that he considered her a restriction on his rather questionable activities.

The day passed uneventfully. The hallway clock was chiming eight o'clock when a light touch of Rosalie's arm made her start. She was going up to her room early, as Lucy had already retired with a headache. In the mellow light of the candle she saw the cowering figure of one of the kitchen-maids.

'If you please, Mistress,' she whispered, looking nervously around. 'I'll help 'ee.'

Rosalie smiled. She bent towards the girl, saying in a low voice, 'Come to my room, then no one will know.'

The girl followed quickly, overwhelmed at being invited into the room of her mistress's guest. Rosalie placed her candle down carefully, knocking off the cold wax that had fallen on to her hand. She indicated to the girl that she should sit on the chair near the fire. The girl shuffled over, perching so near the edge of the chair that she almost fell off.

'Sit back and be comfortable,' Rosalie scolded gently. Her own few servants were respectful to her, but they were also her friends. She was not used to this cringing fear that the servants of Trevia seemed to have.

'Now, how can you help me?' she asked, seating herself on another chair, warming her hands by the glowing coals.

The girl's eyes darted around nervously, as if she expected someone to pounce from the shadows the moment she spoke.

''Tis a cottage I know,' she said at last, her voice so faint it was barely audible.

'Could you take me there?' Rosalie asked, getting her purse. 'Here's half a guinea. I have another for you if you do.'

The girl's eyes widened at the sight of so much money. 'Tonight?' she asked in amazement, her voice more bold.

'Yes, now if possible.'

The girl sat still, her mind slowly turning

over the possibility. 'Aye, I could take 'ee,' she said at last, looking intently at the money in her hand. ' 'Tis deep in mud outside, Mistress,' she added, her eyes now slowly absorbing every inch of her hostess's fine gown.

'I'll change quickly,' Rosalie said, getting out her oldest gown. 'Go and fetch your cloak.'

The girl hurried off, returning a few minutes later, her face flushed with excitement.

There was no moon when the girl led Rosalie along the narrow drive. They had not brought a lantern, thinking it better not to do so. Maintaining secrecy was essential. Gradually their eyes became more accustomed to the darkness. The black shadow of the stone hedge loomed beside them, guiding their steps.

The girl was more confident out of the house, feeling the importance of her task, imparting information on herself and her family more freely.

'My father's a quarry man,' she said proudly. 'He works at Delabole, lifting the slate.'

Rosalie expressed suitable praise that being a quarry man seemed to merit. The girl chatted on, delighted to have such an interested listener.

At the gate, Rosalie lifted her skirts high to wade through the water that had collected there. She muttered a curse that her brothers would pay for the discomfiture that she had to endure. The dampness crept slowly up her legs;

a feeling to which she was not accustomed.

The slate doorstep outside the cottage was a welcome refuge from the miry earth. When the door was opened, a lamp was held to their faces. When Annie Pearce was recognised they were admitted without comment. The door shut quickly behind them. The stone floor was bare slate. When Rosalie saw the condition of her skirts she understood why. The rich Indian carpets on her own floors would serve no useful purpose here.

The woman who had admitted them looked weary; her hair was grey, but her age indeterminable. Rosalie apologised for the late hour, but the woman waved her words away, laughing.

'We keep late hours yere,' she said. Then she frowned at Annie, tilting her head to the side expectantly. 'Well, Annie Pearce, an' why d'you bring a lady to my house at this hour?'

Annie explained, so hurriedly that the words tumbled over each other. The woman was little the wiser when she had finished.

Rosalie smiled. Annie was trying so hard to earn her guinea.

'I will explain, if I may,' she said. The woman bade her sit down and take a cup of tea. She took the kettle from the fire and poured water into a large brown teapot. Throughout the time that Rosalie spoke the woman was silent. She weighed in her mind the risk she would be taking if she admitted that her three sons were out smuggling tonight. I could ask, she thought. There'd be no harm in askin'. She took note in her mind. Two boys, foreigners from over the bridge.

A second cup of tea was drunk before she spoke; still doubtful, still not trusting, but wanting to help this young woman who seemed to have gone to so much trouble already.

'I'll try to help 'ee,' she said slowly. 'I'll ask. If I've news of your brothers, I'll tell 'ee.'

Rosalie beamed, her eyes sparkled with hope. 'When will you know?' she cried eagerly. 'When may I come to see you again?'

The woman shook her head and smiled; she crossed the room to pile more peat on to the dying fire. 'You'll not come by day,' she warned. 'Come at this hour tomorrow. I may've news for 'ee. But I promise 'ee naught,' she said firmly, taking up the lantern as if indicating to her visitors that it was time to leave. Rosalie reached for her purse: the woman put a restraining hand on her arm. 'I'll take no payment,' she said, 'I've given 'ee naught.'

Safely back in her own room again, Rosalie changed her clothes. Annie Pearce took off her own wet frock and stockings, and obediently laid them by the fire to dry. Rosalie placed an iron pot of water on the fire to heat. When it was warm, she instructed the girl to wash her own mud-caked legs.

Once warm and dry again, Annie Pearce

gave a quick curtsy and closed the door softly behind her. Rosalie sighed. She made up the fire, then climbed wearily into the large four-poster. At last, she felt a sense of achievement. It could not be too difficult to find two teenage boys with such obviously different accents and manners. Surely she would soon be home again. Back amongst the warmth and devotion of her own servants.

CHAPTER THREE

When morning came, Lucy Trevia sent her groom into Camelford to make enquiries on Rosalie's behalf. Lucy was playing the pianoforte, a recent gift from Hugh Trevia to his wife. To ease his conscience, Rosalie concluded. The day was dry. A high wind had done much to disperse the floods and dry out the mud.

Rosalie was restless. How she wished it was time to go to the cottage again. Lucy had tried hard to think of ways of finding the boys, but her suggestions were mostly unrealistic, showing her scant knowledge of the world of smuggling.

She was playing a minuet when Rosalie noticed that the drawing-room door was slightly ajar. A small face peered in. As Rosalie recognised Annie Pearce, the girl put up a beckoning finger, then disappeared.

'I think I'll fetch a book, Lucy,' Rosalie said, calmly opening the door. 'I'll not be long.' She went out into the hall, but could see no one. She climbed the stairs, glancing continually around. There was still no sign of the girl. It was in her room that she found her, hiding behind the door, screwing her apron in her hands with agitation.

'What are you doing there?' Rosalie asked in surprise.

'If you please, Mistress, I've a message for 'ee, but no one must hear,' the girl said in a whisper.

Rosalie nodded. She checked her dressing-room for her chambermaid, but it was empty.

The girl crept nearer, still whispering. 'Your brothers, Mistress. They'm on the *Peacock*.'

'The *Peacock*, a ship? Where will I find her?'

'She be coming in tonight. Her boats'll come in Kylen Tek.'

'Is that far? How many miles? At what hour?' The flood of questions made the frightened girl more nervous than ever. She drew back, startled and confused.

Rosalie gradually determined, however, that the boat was arriving at two o'clock on the following morning with a cargo of gin and rum from Roscoff. It was thought possible that her brothers might be sent on shore with the boats. She thanked the girl, giving her a kerchief of embroidered Nottingham lace. She suspected that too many half-guineas might go to the girl's head. She would get herself in trouble if it were suspected that she were passing on information.

Rosalie returned to the drawing-room, book in hand.

'The weather is much improved, Lucy,' she said. 'Would it not be possible for you to show me the sea today? I'm so impatient to see this large expanse of water.'

Lucy beamed, springing to her feet. 'An excellent idea, Rosalie. I think we could ride after noon. I'll instruct the groom to have horses ready. He's returned, with no news of your brothers, I fear.'

Rosalie had decided it was useless to expect help from the servants of Trevia. They were too afraid.

She had no illusions about her own bravery, but she had no alternative but to go to the cove herself. If her brothers might be there, she must at least try to see them. Her horse was in a lively mood as they took the narrow bridle path to the coast. He shied at the slightest excuse. She was almost thrown twice. Lucy was most concerned, full of apologies, swearing to chastise the groom severely for his choice of mount for her guest.

Rosalie just laughed, a frisky horse was the least of her worries at the moment. She prided herself that riding was one of her better accomplishments. Robert had seen to that—

Robert, the expert on any horse. Yet when she thought of him now, she admitted a sense of disappointment, for she realised that in telling him she was going to Cornwall, she had secretly hoped that he would come with her. She had been disillusioned. Robert had done no more than write letters to find the boys. She would have preferred it had he ridden off after them, like knights of old. She laughed to herself; her sense of valour was a little outdated. A family failing, no doubt, as her brothers were proving.

'We're near the sea, Rosalie. Can you not smell the seaweed?' Lucy's voice brought her back to reality. She sniffed the air and acknowledged a strange new smell.

'We must dismount here, Rosalie,' Lucy called. 'It would not be wise to go near the cliff edge on horseback. Especially with that spirited bay.'

Rosalie bit her lip to stop herself from laughing. The pun on words was so apt. If Lucy only knew the real reason she had asked to be shown this particular cove.

She tethered her horse, then followed Lucy cautiously. The wind was fresh against her face, her heart beating fast as she stepped forward to get her first glance of the Atlantic Ocean. She gasped. Her eyes widened with amazement. The sea was so large, so noisy. She had read so much about it, but never had she imagined the beautiful sight before her now.

She turned to Lucy, her face radiant with delight. The fact that she must find her way here in the dark completely obliterated from her mind.

'Oh, Lucy,' she cried, 'it's magnificent. Can we not climb down? Can we not walk to the water?'

Lucy laughed. 'It's not meet for a lady to do such a thing, Rosalie, but—' She hesitated. 'If you really wish it. There's no one to see us. There is a path leading down over here.'

She crossed the turf, her steps light, the excitement that Rosalie had felt infecting her, too. 'I dare not think what Hugh would say,' she laughed.

'Hugh is not here, Lucy, and why should men always decide for us what we may or may not do?' Rosalie said indignantly.

They trod carelessly over the sand, laughing at their own footprints. Rosalie walked right to the water's edge, her face still glowing, her eyes shining. She bent her slender body and pressed her fingers into the damp sand, then she leaned towards the lapping waves and ran her hands gently through the water. When she straightened up, she put a wet finger into her mouth, then she laughed.

'It really is salty, Lucy. I did—' She stopped and stared out to sea. 'Is that a ship, Lucy?' she cried, her eyes resting on the billowing white sails of a schooner. 'The kind of ship that my brothers may be on?'

Lucy nodded and smiled. 'She looks so frail from here, does she not?'

The sight of the schooner was enthralling enough, but it reminded Rosalie of her real purpose in visiting the cove. She turned from the sea, her eyes scanning the cliffs and the caves for a suitable hiding place. And she found one.

Throughout the ride home, Rosalie noted the direction they took, mentally storing landmarks she might recognise in the dark. A farmhouse, a steep hill, the ford through the River Allen. She dare not take a horse at night, for the stableboys slept with them and would surely wake.

It was early that evening when Rosalie excused herself and retired to bed. She had a long, tiring walk ahead of her, yet she dare not sleep. The time passed slowly, dragging, until at last the hands of the china clock on the bedside table reached midnight and Rosalie dressed. The house was silent. An owl hooted in the trees, another answered some distance away. As Rosalie's foot touched a creaking stair she was quite sure it was bound to wake the whole sleeping household. She held her breath; stood motionless, listening; nothing stirred. The September night was cold as she stepped out, dressed in her brother Peter's clothes.

She kept in the shadows, the deep band of black given to her by the high Cornish stone hedge. The sparse trees gave little shelter, their wind-bowed branches shining silver in the moonlight. The bridle path was rough, she stumbled often over dead branches, over granite stones from the wall, scratching her face on brambles, then getting up quickly from the damp grass, seething with annoyance at her own stupidity. The full moon lit the way ahead with startling clarity. A horseman came by her once and she crouched terrified in the shadow till he had passed.

It was four miles to the sea from Trevia House. Rosalie hoped desperately that she had given herself enough time. She had assumed that the men would go to the beach well before the ship was due. She must at all costs be there before them. Her clothing felt strange. She had never before worn breeches, but her gowns and petticoats would have made hiding so much harder. The night sky was clear, the air strangely still, when she reached at last the edge of the open downs. Her body ached with weariness. Her breath came hot and fast from hurrying. She crouched down, listening intently; she heard only the unceasing roar of the sea as it tossed itself carelessly on to the moon-whitened sand below her.

Keeping low, she crept warily towards the edge of the cliff, knowing well that the stark white light that came uninterrupted from the sky might easily spotlight her moving figure. Her boots slipped on the path, made treacherous by the dampness of night. Her fingers ached as she gripped the cold rocks to steady herself.

About half-way down, a wide ledge dipped into shadow. She crawled along it and made herself as comfortable as she was able, assuring for herself a clear view of the beach below. Then she waited; and she waited; and she waited. At last, faintly, doubtfully, increasingly clear, she heard the thud of hoofbeats, the whinny of horses as they halted above her.

Eventually she counted twenty men, climbing down past her, cursing under their breath, their heavy footsteps striking the slate like castanets. They came in twos, in threes, or alone. Some had ridden, some had walked. They stood on the beach waiting, idly kicking at the sand with their boots.

A fierce lantern came swinging down the path. A buzz of approval rose and fell.

''Tis time, lads,' the lantern-holder called. 'She's there. I'll signal she.' He swung the lantern to and fro until, faintly past the Mackerel rocks, Rosalie saw a tiny answering light and her eyes picked out the gently swaying form of a cutter.

The men moved restlessly, thrusting their hands into their pockets, or swinging their arms to keep warm. The tide was high, the beach where Rosalie had stood earlier now deep in water. She strained her eyes across the shimmering sea until she saw dark figures, bending their bodies as they rowed, coming nearer and nearer. Soon she heard the intermittent creaking of working oars. Murmurs of gladness came from the men. They moved quickly forward, preparing to haul in the loaded boats.

As Rosalie watched, the moonlit beach held a strangely breathtaking scene, sharpened acutely by the deep shadows, by the black emptiness of the dank caves and rocky crannies. The men worked hard, unloading the kegs from the boats, tossing them easily on to their shoulders and striding quickly into the now lamp-lit entrance of the largest cave. They went deep inside, the length of their journey surprising to Rosalie.

As she watched, she almost heard her father's voice as he read stories about scenes like this. Had it not been for the cold, numb aching of her muscles, she might have believed it a dream.

'John Treleven?' The shout made her start, but she saw it was only the man with the lantern calling to a watcher on the cliff top. His answer came swift and sure.

'All clear, Mansell.'

Mansell nodded his approval and waved the working men on. Every now and then he would glance out to sea, watching the small boats as they went backwards and forwards with their cargoes, then up at the moon, as if cursing its presence and wishing for a good sou'wester that might bring cloud into the night sky. Rosalie froze, moulded as if part of the rock that hid her. The smell of wet seaweed and the lichen filled her nostrils. She scarcely breathed, terrified that the slightest movement might send shale scurrying down the cliff, alerting the men to her presence.

It had not taken her long to acknowledge sadly that her brothers were not amongst them. She had stayed, half-fearful to leave, half-hoping that she might catch an unguarded conversation that might give her reason to have hope of finding them. The boats were almost empty now. The men talked amongst themselves, recounting with great pleasure to the sailors how they had sent a handful of men to another cove to lay a false trail for the coastguard at Boscastle. A keg of rum had been opened. The men drank thirstily, using anything to drink out of, including their hands.

The boats began to leave. A chill wind blew up suddenly from the sea. Rosalie shivered. Then, without warning, a seagull flew from behind her head, its flapping wings and screeching call piercing the close silence around her. Startled, she tried to stifle the cry that left her lips, but as her hand muffled the sound she knew that it was too late. Her movement had sent pebbles bouncing down, clattering a jig on their way. She saw the upturned faces, heard rough voices shout.

Quickly she turned to climb as footsteps came behind her on the path. Her limbs were stiffened by the cold, but she climbed as fast as she could. Her body was tense, her heart beating fast with the excited anticipation of danger. She reached the top. In a moment of achievement her body relaxed. Glancing hurriedly behind her, she saw a figure almost on her. She heard him shout to the watcher on the cliff who had started in pursuit.

'I'll get him.'

Rosalie ran, her body bathed in an icy sweat as the salt wind gusted and stung her cheeks, its force grabbing her forward, then dropping her as easily. She gained the rough slope to the bridle path. The stone wall seemed higher than before; she scrambled over, uttering an involuntary cry as she fell heavily on the other side. She did not hear the man behind her and sighed a little with relief, forcing her weary body onwards.

A rough hand grabbed her shoulder and threw her to the ground. She struggled and fought, seeking to wrench herself from his grip. She had almost freed herself when he grabbed at her clothes. The coat pulled open; the shirt tore. In the moonlight, he saw that this was no mischievous boy shaking at his feet, but a full-grown woman.

He knelt down beside her, staring into her frightened eyes, still disbelieving. As the moonlight crossed his face Rosalie saw that he was young. She allowed herself hope.

'I trust I've not hurt you,' he said at last, keeping his voice low, 'but I thought—'

'I know and I don't blame you. I meant no harm. I was only seeking my brothers whom I've lost.'

He shook his head and smiled. '' Tis well 'twas I caught you, Mistress,' he said.

They heard a voice calling. His face grew anxious, his dark eyes betraying his fears. 'You must go quickly,' he said hurriedly. 'I'll say you escaped me—and indeed you almost did,' he added with a laugh. He held out his arm and helped her to her feet, the hint of laughter still in his eyes. 'I'd see you safe home, but I've a mind 'tis better for you I return to the beach.'

She smiled her thanks, then ran. He watched her go before he returned to his companions. As he climbed down to the beach he cursed loudly that the young rascal had outwitted him. He thought it no more than a young lad with adventure in his heart who would not dare to tell anyone of his nightly escapade.

When, exhausted and footsore, Rosalie reached her bed she was still shivering with the cold. She cupped her hands around the candle flame to take a little of the aching from them, for the fire was black and dead. The room was cold. Undressing quickly, she sank gratefully under the bedclothes. Sleep did not come easily to her. Her mind was too much alive, reliving her fortuitous escape, remembering the startled face of the young smuggler when he had discovered her to be other than a boy. She was disheartened at finding no sign of Peter or Ben; yet, secretly, she felt a strange exhilaration. A feeling for adventure that she had never before experienced.

CHAPTER FOUR

Determined to trace the *Peacock* to her home port, Rosalie rode out each day from Trevia. She visited the harbour at Boscastle, the bays of Port Isaac, Port Gaverne and Trebarwith; no one, it seemed, had the courage to help her. She was greeted everywhere with silent tongues and suspicious eyes. Her only lead to the whereabouts of her brothers was so illusive that even the woman in the cottage at Trevia had changed her mind, reminding Rosalie that she was, after all, a foreigner. Every evening she returned, exhausted from riding, disillusioned by her own lack of achievement; more afraid each day that she would never again see the reckless boys that she had loved so much.

The noonday sun was behind her as she turned her mount from The Clease into Fore Street; as she made a last bid to win the confidence of the people of Camelford. As her horse descended the hill, she turned him into the yard of the King's Arms. She had to begin again somewhere. The landlord was polite, but told her nothing. She led her horse slowly down the hill, ignoring the stares of the few townfolk who stood leaning in the doorways of their small timber-framed houses.

The smell of new warm bread told her that she was passing the bakehouse. It was a refreshing change from the odour of pigs that seemed to always hang around the town. A scraggy-looking sow came squealing out of one of the houses, frightening the horse. A small, dark-haired man came running out of the blacksmith's, offering to steady the horse, but Rosalie had already tightened the rein and her horse came forward steadily, acknowledging his mistress. She thanked the man, then took the horse into the yard of the Bedford Arms, giving him into the care of the ostler.

Enquiries here, at the White Hart and at the shops and forges were fruitless. Visits to the large cornmill over the river and the cloth factory revealed little. Some people seemed to have vague recollections of her brothers passing through the town, but no one knew where they went. No one, it seemed, cared. Rosalie was beaten. Peter and Ben seemed to have vanished. The *Peacock* had done the same. Surely someone must know where they were. Even the constables at Camelford had advised her to go home as soon as she had arrived. The staunch resoluteness with which she had started the search was fading. Rosalie saw only defeat.

Aimlessly, she turned from the narrow street through an archway between the houses, and found herself beside the river. The River Camel was shallow, the multi-coloured stone that made its bed reminded her of a Roman mosaic. As she walked beside it, she watched it curving ahead of her, hurrying noisily, babbling over large rocks to make scores of tiny waterfalls.

Rosalie sighed. Never before had she felt such defeat. She had thought it would be so easy to find the boys. A blackbird winged its way down from the top of the tall rowans that swayed above her. Autumn came later in Cornwall. She had noticed the trees were still well covered. The lowest branches bowed gracefully over the river, their shadows dancing on the water between the dashes of silver sunlight. The tree trunks were ringed thickly with ivy; the herringbone wall that she reached now was clad in the same dark shining leaves.

'You mustn't look sad on such a handsome day, Mistress Harvey.'

Rosalie drew back, startled. She stared at the tall young man who had stepped into her path through an opening in the wall. He was dressed in leather breeches and a clean white shirt, an emerald-green kerchief at his throat. His thick black hair curled to his shoulders.

She was about to turn away when he spoke

again.

'There's no cause for alarm, Mistress. I only wish to speak with you. I fear you don't remember me.'

Rosalie looked back towards him. The black hair, the dark eyes. The dark eyes began to laugh.

Then she gasped. 'Why, it's my smuggler!' she cried.

He burst out laughing, shaking his head. 'I've no objection if you call me yours, Mistress, but if we were not alone and you called me a smuggler I'd be thrown into Bodmin Gaol.'

Rosalie blushed; she smoothed down her skirts nervously. 'I did not mean to offend you, sir, but I did not know you at first. You wish to speak with me?'

He nodded. 'Shall we walk a little, lest we be overheard?' He turned, walking beside her. 'I understand,' he said, 'you've two young rascals for brothers.'

'Indeed I do, and my efforts to find them are completely hopeless. I'm at my wits' end to know where they've gone.'

The man stopped for a moment, watching her closely, leaning his arm on the wall. 'Then will you let me help you?' he asked.

Rosalie's face beamed. She felt like flinging her arms round his neck and kissing him, so great was the relief. She maintained her dignity, however, held out her hand and smiled.

'Your offer is most gratefully accepted, sir. I've found very little help so far.'

He took her hand, bowed his head and kissed it lightly. Not the action she would have expected from a smuggler.

They walked a little further downriver until the path ended. A rough-hewn plank was thrown across the water to the other side, where the path continued. The man looked at her expectantly, but seeing the doubt in her face, he crossed first, showing her it was safe. Then he came back a short way and, holding out his hand, he steadied her across.

'If I'm to help you,' he said as they walked on, 'I'll need to know a little of your brothers.'

Rosalie nodded and smiled. 'Indeed you must. But, first, will you not tell me your name or I may be tempted to call you "my smuggler" again?'

The man laughed, then bending down he picked up a pebble and skimmed it across the water. 'My name's Michael,' he said simply.

'Well, Michael, my brother Peter is sixteen. He's tall for his age. His hair, the colour of mine. He's well read. Remarkably good at mathematics.'

'They've not been to sea before, Mistress Harvey?'

'They have visited the coast with my father, but never boarded a ship. Their enthusiasm for the life comes from books.'

'Which no doubt show it only in a pleasing light.'

'I fear so. Do you read, Michael?'

'At every opportunity. I'd a craving to study navigation as a boy. This made me learn to read. I've but few books, but I know them well.'

'And what books do you have?'

He paused thoughtfully. '*Robinson Crusoe*. I enjoy Shakespeare, but I've only three of his plays.'

Their path was blocked now by a stone wall. Fallen in front of it was a gnarled and twisted tree trunk. Michael pointed to the tree. 'Shall we sit awhile. If Mistress Harvey continues walking she'll reach Pencarrow and her horse'll find its own way home.'

Rosalie nodded, laughing. She sat herself down, her heart racing a little, overwhelmed with relief. Then she spoke suddenly, her face puzzled. 'How did you know my name? I've not told you. Indeed, I could have been any woman, dressed as I was.'

Michael climbed higher on the fallen tree, using the branches as an armchair. He raised his eyebrows and smiled.

'Pray give me credit for knowing a lady when she speaks, Mistress.' He shrugged. 'A few enquiries here and there. It didn't take long to find Mistress Harvey, very intent on asking awkward questions.'

Rosalie felt the colour flood to her cheeks.

'Your enquiries yielded much better than mine, Michael. I've discovered nothing.'

He frowned. 'I've certain advantages. In Cornwall we don't trust easy. Life's hard. Freedom precious, yet easy to lose.' He smiled, then went on, 'Tell me, is your second brother like Peter?'

'He's smaller, of course. Twelve years, merely a child, the same fair hair. He reads quite well, but he's more talented in drawing than mathematics.'

'A boy of twelve's not a child in Cornwall, Mistress Harvey. He'd've worked three years at least. As I know children do in your part of the country, in mills and mines.'

Rosalie felt uncomfortable. She answered slowly, 'Yes, I believe we've children in my father's mill.'

'Your father owns a mill?'

'My parents are dead, my brothers and I own a mill.'

Michael was silent, thinking deeply. He broke twigs from the trunk and, snapping them in his fingers, he tossed them into the river. Then he glanced behind him and up at the sky. 'The sun's well over the turnpike,' he said. 'Is it not time you returned to Trevia for luncheon?'

Rosalie nodded and got carefully to her feet, removing the twigs that were caught in her gown. 'How will I find you, to know if you've news of my brothers?'

He laughed, then jumped down from his

comfortable seat.

'I'll find you, Mistress Harvey,' he said with a slight bow. Then his face grew serious, his hands rested lightly on his hips. 'If I'm to help you,' he said, 'you'll make me a vow.'

Rosalie turned to face him. 'What kind of vow?' she asked, puzzled.

'You'll vow to me that you'll not go to the coves by night again,' he said sternly, then added with a twinkle in his eye, 'unless I take you myself.'

Rosalie felt affronted. Why should she make such a vow to this man? 'I am mistress of my own will, sir. I'll make no such vow,' she said angrily.

'Then I can't help you,' he said quickly, shrugging his shoulders.

Rosalie's anger grew. How dare he try to make bargains with her, and he a smuggler at that. 'You think I'll make reports to the preventive officers,' she retorted.

He turned towards her abruptly. He stared at her face with amazement. 'I said no such thing, nor even minded it.' His voice softened and he went on, 'I've seen and heard of the diligence with which you've sought your brothers. I respect your courage greatly. When I caught you, disguised as a boy, you were in more danger than I think you realise.'

'I'm aware that you probably saved my life. For this I thank you.'

''Twould be more than your life that you

lost had I taken you to the beach. 'Tis why I ask you to make the vow. I'll not have you in such danger again.' His black eyes flashed angrily now, but Rosalie realised with astonishment that the anger was not for her but the memory of her closeness to peril.

She put her hand impetuously on his arm. 'I beg your pardon. I misjudged your motive. I'll not go to the sea at night.' Then she smiled, adding, 'Unless you take me.'

His face relaxed and he returned the smile. ' 'Twill be a few days before I've news of your brothers. Be patient. I'll find them,' he said.

They had reached the primitive bridge. He helped her across as before, then stopped.

'I'll go no further with you, Mistress Harvey. 'Tis better that I'm not seen talking to you. If we meet in the town, please pass me by without a glance.'

Rosalie nodded her understanding. 'Thank you for your kindness; my mind is greatly relieved to know you'll help me, but tell me, does not Michael have a second name or do you not trust me with it?'

'Pendeen, Mistress Harvey. Michael Pendeen. And if I've two names, then so must you,' he said with a laugh.

Rosalie thought frantically. Should she really allow this man to call her by her Christian name? She looked at his face and involuntarily into his dark shining eyes.

Then she heard herself saying quietly, 'My

name is Rosalie.'

The smile spread from his eyes; he gave a slight bow. 'A pretty name indeed, Mistress Rosalie. I'll see you again. Good day.' Then he turned quickly and was gone.

When Rosalie arrived back at Trevia, Lucy was waiting for her, eager to show her the new polonaise and morning gown she had had made in preparation for a hoped-for visit to London. Rosalie admired them dutifully, her mind hardly tuned to elegant gowns at the moment. Her thoughts were racing, running in circles. Then she thought of Robert, and they steadied.

When luncheon was over, she sat down to write to him. It was the first letter. She knew it was unkind of her. She had promised to write early. She had decided, however, to make Robert worry a little. He was even unaware of her safe arrival. She wondered how much he really cared. How much was the habit of years. She wrote briefly, saying that she had not yet found the boys, but telling him nothing of the difficulties she had encountered. Telling him nothing of Michael Pendeen.

Lucy was surprised at Rosalie's sudden cheerfulness. She enjoyed immensely having her guest stay at Trevia. Although she wished Rosalie to find her brothers, she was not too unhappy at the problems, for it meant that Rosalie would stay longer. They walked in the garden for the afternoon, Rosalie smiling and gay, able for once to give her full attention to her hostess. The responsibility for her brothers had lifted a little. Michael Pendeen had taken it away with him.

CHAPTER FIVE

The rain suddenly began throwing itself at the earth as if it had a time limit to beat. It was ten o'clock in the morning four days later. Rosalie sat reading in the drawing-room, listening to the rain; glad to be inside by a warm fire. A knock on the door heralded Blueitt, who announced somewhat wearily that there was a young gentleman wishing to see Mistress Harvey.

Rosalie's heart stopped beating for a second, fluttered, then pounded furiously. She told herself firmly to stop being so foolish, set her book down slowly and rose to her feet. She was a little surprised that Michael Pendeen had come to the front door at Trevia, not that it mattered to her... It occurred to her suddenly that it might not be Michael. It might even be one of her brothers. She flew out of the room, almost knocking over the astonished butler, ran into the hall, then stopped dead.

'Robert!' she exclaimed. 'What are you doing here?'

Robert stood with water running in channels

down his cloak. It fell in tiny pools on the floor. He ran a wet glove over his dripping face and stared at Rosalie. He had expected her to be overjoyed to see him. Blueitt assisted him off with his cloak and hat, then took them away to dry. Robert removed his soaking gloves, then wiped his face with a kerchief from his pocket.

'Are you not pleased to see me, Rosalie?' he asked, with dismay.

Rosalie pulled herself together quickly. 'Why, Robert!' she exclaimed, forcing a smile. 'Of course I'm delighted to see you. Just a little surprised.'

'I've been greatly worried since you left, Rosalie. You did not write as you promised. I had thoughts of highwaymen, all manner of danger for you to be in. You cannot imagine the sleepless nights I've had.'

Rosalie allowed herself to gloat a little. Robert had been concerned about her.

'I have written to you, Robert. Four days since,' she said.

He nodded. 'I see. I would have left for London before your letter arrived.' He looked at her with admiration in his eyes. 'You look well, Rosalie. Have you news of Peter and Ben?'

Rosalie frowned. 'I am well, but I've no news. Come, I'll introduce you to Lucy Trevia.'

'Is Hugh not here?'

'He's in London, but Lucy and I are great

friends.' She led the way, still puzzled at her own reaction. She had been annoyed to find Robert standing there, yet a few days before she had wished he would come.

Lucy, as always, was delighted to meet a new acquaintance. 'You will stay here, of course, Mr James,' she insisted.

The servants were summoned, a room prepared for him and a man sent to the King's Arms to bring his luggage. Robert was glad enough to change his wet clothes when the man returned.

Lucy cornered Rosalie as soon as Robert had gone. 'However could you refuse such a marvellous man, Rosalie? He's so handsome, and he's travelled all this way because he feared for your safety!' she exclaimed.

Rosalie laughed. She supposed Robert was handsome. She had never considered it before. Robert was just Robert, he always had been. She wished he had not come. She was enjoying a new-found freedom. Lucy, always anxious to please, found her guest's slightly wayward behaviour exciting, a new adventure in her dreary existence.

Robert, alone in his room, was puzzled. He had come to Cornwall convinced that in a very short time he would have found the boys and have them and their sister safely in a north-east bound coach. Rosalie's refusal of his offer of marriage had certainly hurt his pride. He had soon dismissed it, however, as entirely due to her brothers' misdemeanours. He had decided it was time he took her in hand and married her. He was rather surprised at how much he had missed her. He had had great difficulty in restraining himself when they parted. When Rosalie had rushed into the hall at Trevia, he had been about to discard the etiquette of courtship and take her into his arms. Then she had stopped. He had been confused, completely disillusioned. Had it been disappointment he had seen in her eyes? Robert was unsure of himself once more.

When luncheon was over, Rosalie felt restless. Lucy, delighted to hear that Robert had been in London, insisted he tell her all the news. He had not encountered her husband, which surprised her. Robert, knowing Hugh's reputation, veered off the subject quickly. Rosalie listened absentmindedly. She had little interest in the social activities at the best of times, even less at the moment. She plied her needle into her embroidery with the same lack of enthusiasm.

The rain had stopped as suddenly as it had begun. The sky was clearing; a brilliant rainbow spanned the moor.

'I think, if you will excuse me, I'll take a walk in the garden,' she said, putting her embroidery carefully down on a side table. Robert rose slightly as if he was about to offer to accompany her, but Lucy was entreating him to tell her more about London. Robert sat down again and Rosalie went out alone.

She avoided the sodden lawns, keeping to the paths in her endeavour to get as far away from the house as possible. The air smelt so beautifully fresh after the rain, the fragrance of the late roses filling her nostrils as she walked beneath the long arbour. A pale sun was beginning to spread its warmth, making the tree boughs shine with the wet. Along the branches, suspended like tiny diamonds, were scores of water droplets glittering in the sunlight. She walked on, shuddering a little as water dripped on her head when she walked through the deep arch of the yew hedge. She crossed the paved Italian garden to where there was a carved oak garden seat. She sat down, ignoring the dampness of the wood on her gown.

Robert's presence had reminded her acutely just how much she missed her brothers. They got into scrapes continually, but how she missed their laughter, their teasing, and she worried continually about their health, their fitness for such as a life at sea. Would they survive such severity? How she wished they would run into her arms, calling her Rosie, as they were wont to do when they wished to taunt her. She sighed wearily. Life had seemed so well organised, so peaceful until the boys had run away. Now it was confused, so unsure. Even her marriage to Robert, which she had accepted as inevitable one day, seemed unlikely, even undesirable. She leaned back on to the seat and sighed again.

A rustling in the shrubs behind her made her turn; then she heard her name whispered softly. This time she was sure. It was Michael Pendeen. She got unhurriedly to her feet and, lifting her skirts, she walked down a narrow gravel path through the trees.

He was sitting perched on top of the stone wall that formed the boundary of the Trevia gardens. He smiled when he saw her and sprang down from the wall.

'Good day, Mistress Rosalie. I'd a mind you might take a walk now the rain's ceased.'

'Good day to you, Michael. Do you have news?' she asked eagerly.

'A little.' His face became tense, and she knew it was not the news she had hoped for.

'Your brothers were on the *Peacock* when she sailed from Breton. I'd hoped that if they came ashore they'd have remained so for a while, but 'tis not so. They took employment on a packet schooner with a charted cargo.'

Rosalie looked up at him with dismay in her eyes.

He smiled. ''Tis not the end of the world, Mistress Rosalie. We'll find 'em. I've not been able to determine the schooner yet. When I do, I'll check her owner's charter list.' He looked anxiously towards the house for a moment, but they were well hidden. 'Will you come here tomorrow at the same time?'

Rosalie nodded.

'You'll come even if 'tis raining?' he asked with a look of amusement in his dark eyes.

Rosalie raised her eyebrows with indignation. 'I'm not afraid of a little rain,' she said.

He laughed. 'Indeed I know you're not. I'll be here tomorrow.'

'Do not go, Michael. I've something for you. Some books. Would you like to borrow them?'

He was obviously surprised at her offer. 'I would indeed. I'll wait.'

Rosalie returned to the house, trying hard not to hurry. Her heart was racing again, which she found disconcerting. The books were in the drawing-room, a little inconvenient as Robert and Lucy were still there. She entered the room trying to look calm and unflustered.

'I have just remembered I wished to look up a quotation. I'll do it in the garden.'

Robert looked dangerously as if he were going to follow her, so she gave him an extra warm smile. 'I'll not be long, Robert. I'll be quicker if I'm alone.'

He looked disappointed, but sat down. Rosalie picked up the small pile of books, gave him another purposeful smile, then returned to the shrubbery. Michael had vanished. She called his name and he appeared from behind a tall evergreen. 'I'd a mind your guest might accompany you,' he said.

'My guest?' Rosalie asked.

Michael grimaced. 'Aye, the young man who came in last evening on the stage. I assume he's a friend of yours. He asked for Trevia at the King's Arms.'

Rosalie found the colour rising in her cheeks; she kept her face down as if checking the books. 'Yes, Robert is a friend of mine. He came to see if I'd found my brothers.'

'You're to wed him?' Michael enquired.

The question was so direct that Rosalie looked up in surprise. 'I—er—don't know,' she said, flustered. 'He wants me to, but I don't know.'

'I see,' Michael said slowly. 'You're not sure you wish it.'

'No ... Are you married, Michael?' The possibility had not occurred to her before. She suddenly needed to know.

Michael threw back his head and laughed. 'Indeed I'm not. I've only lived six-and-twenty years; there's time enough for marriage.'

Rosalie held out the books, glad of an excuse to change the subject. 'You may borrow any of these. I hope they'll be to your liking. You mentioned Shakespeare, but I don't know which you've read.'

Michael took the books, handling them as if they were fragile china. He read the titles slowly, his eyes shining with delight. '*Richard the Third. Hamlet.* I saw *Hamlet* by the players at the White Hart at Lans'n. These I've always wished to read.' He looked at Rosalie, his face anxious. 'May I really borrow all of these?' he asked.

'Why of course. You may keep them until—well, until I go home.'

'You're very kind, Mistress Rosalie. I'll take great care of them.'

'Rosalie!' Robert's voice came to them, suddenly, loudly.

Michael grinned. 'I'd best make myself vanish,' he whispered. 'I'll see you tomorrow.' He climbed the wall quickly and was hidden amongst the trees.

Rosalie crept back along the gravel path. She peered cautiously out between a laurel and a honeysuckle. Robert was walking slowly around the garden with a distinctly baffled expression on his face. She stood quite still, waited for him to pass, then hurried in the opposite direction. By the time Robert re-entered the hall, Rosalie was gracefully descending the stairs.

'Have you been into the garden, Robert?' she enquired, stifling a giggle. 'I've just been to my room to return the books.'

Robert's face relaxed a little, but still showed some doubts. Rosalie was behaving in a most unusual manner. I'm deuced sure she is hiding something, he thought.

'I wanted to talk with you, Rosalie, alone,' he said.

Rosalie smiled up at him serenely, fluttering her eyelashes a little. 'Oh, did you, Robert,' she said. 'Come into the garden room; we'll be alone there.'

The conversation that followed was strained, Robert trying to find exactly what efforts Rosalie had made to find her brothers, insisting that he must get to work on the search immediately. Rosalie subconsciously resented his questions, unwilling to disclose her failure, yet having a strong desire to keep Michael Pendeen to herself. She was quite sure that Robert's enquiries would meet with the same blank expressions as had her own. Michael would find them, of this she was completely convinced.

Rosalie tried very hard during the rest of the day to be especially nice to Robert. The fact that she had to try at all was a strange emotion in itself. Being nice to Robert was usually just part of her. He went out for most of the evening and all of the following day, getting blank stares to his questions.

The garden was drier when Rosalie parted the bushes again the following afternoon and slipped between them. Michael was there waiting, sitting on the wall as before. When his black eyes met hers she looked away quickly, feeling the colour rush to her cheeks and her heart start to race. She took a long, slow, deep breath. What on earth was the matter with her? She was annoyed at her own behaviour. This man was a servant; but no matter how hard she tried she could only think of him as a man, and a man who attracted her.

Jumping down beside her, he pushed a bramble away from her gown before he spoke.

'Your friend is getting a little angry,' he said.

'You mean Robert?'

'Aye, he's certain he can get any man to work for him. He'll get less help than you did, and that was little enough.'

'Why are people so reluctant to help, Michael? They would be well paid. It's no crime.'

He frowned. 'They're afraid, Mistress Rosalie. Afraid for their lives. You know, your brothers came here of their own free will, they sought employment of their own free will. But the captain of the ship might be accused of kidnapping them, of forcing them to work on his ship, as the press gangs do. If he were so charged, then those who gave information'd be punished by his friends.'

'Are you not afraid then, Michael? Do you not put yourself in danger by helping me?'

He just grinned, then looked up quickly as a shower of leaves came floating gracefully down from a branch above their heads. They fell on to Rosalie's hair and shoulders. Michael laughed as she tried to shake them off. Then he put his hand gently on her hair and plucked off the ones that remained.

'Yesterday it rained water, today it rains leaves,' he said. 'I wonder if 'twill rain mercy tomorrow, or was Portia's world too removed from Cornwall?'

Rosalie's eyes widened. 'You've read *The Merchant of Venice*?' she said.

He nodded. 'Several times.'

'And would you like to live amongst the people of whom you have read?'

He was thoughtful, weighing the question carefully. 'I think not, but I might envy them their clothes sometimes.' He laughed. 'I might envy your friend his fine attire. Not that I could wear it in the life I lead. But perchance I'd like the chance to walk in the garden with you. To discuss Antonio and Bassanio on an open terrace, instead of hidden in the bushes, like a thief stealing your time.' He looked at Rosalie for a moment, then threw back his head in laughter. 'Your Shakespeare gives me notions above my station. I'd best give you my news and be gone.'

'I'd walk in the garden with you, dressed as you are,' Rosalie said slowly, even to her own surprise.

'And would you not care for the stares and sly remarks? You know little of me, but the servants of Trevia know me well.'

Rosalie smiled. 'I've told you before, I'm mistress of my own will. The servants of Trevia do not direct my actions, nor do I care for their opinions. I'm already strange in their eyes, for I ride out alone and do as I please.'

'Does your friend approve?' he asked, his eyes flashing with humour.

'Robert knows me well, but I admit his being here puts some restriction on my actions.' She sighed, then spoke almost to herself. 'I wish he had not come.' Then, remembering that Michael had come for a purpose, she begged him to tell her the news of her brothers.

'Little more,' he said. 'I've the ship's name. She's sailed for Boston in America. Her owners are at Padstow. I'll be away a while, Mistress Rosalie. When I return, I'll go to Padstow. There I'll find if the ship'll return straight to Cornwall or if she's other calls to make. We'll know then how long 'twill be before your brothers return.'

'America is a fearful way off,' Rosalie sighed.

''Tis true, but the captain's a fair-minded man. If they work hard they'll come to no harm from him.'

'Is it far to Padstow, Michael?'

'Half a day's journey.'

'Will you take me with you?' Rosalie was almost as surprised at her own request as was Michael.

He looked at her in amazement, then his gaze fell to her gown, then back to her face. 'I'll go on horseback.'

'I can ride,' she said.

'Bareback? I've no saddles.'

She was less sure now. She hesitated before answering. 'I'll try without a saddle,' she said.

Michael shook his head slowly. 'I'll not take

you as a boy, and your clothes alone would restrict my enquiries. A friend of the Lady Trevia's no friend of the fishermen of Padstow.'

'I could make another gown. One more suitable. Can I not buy such material as your sisters would wear?'

His mouth twisted into a slight smile, then he nodded. ''Tis Camelford market today. They'll sell such cloth. I'm riding there now. Will I buy you some?' There was eagerness in his voice that gave her confidence. At first she had thought he did not want to take her.

''Twould look odd if you ride there yourself,' he went on, then suddenly his face broke into a broad grin. 'You'd likely meet your friend. He's there now, demanding assistance. He offered me a guinea if I'd tell him where to find a smuggler.'

Rosalie laughed. 'Did you tell him he must go to the beach by night and hide amongst the rocks?'

Michael laughed again. He leaned his back against the silver trunk of the birch tree, looking up into the branches. 'I told him that if he returned to Trevia within the hour he'd find one sitting on the wall in the garden.'

'Oh, Michael! You did not?'

He shook his head. 'No, I did not, but I was sorely tempted to do so.'

Rosalie lifted her skirts and walked nearer the wall, with her back to him. 'Then you'll take me to Padstow, if I make a gown?'

He did not answer, but crossed to the wall and leaned on it beside her, his chin resting on his hand as if he was working out every possible angle of such a journey.

'I'll do as you tell me,' she pleaded.

He turned to face her, his eyes, pondering, grave. 'If I can borrow the cart for two days, then I will take you. Do you understand what you're asking? We'll stay one night in my uncle's house. There'll be no servants for you.'

'I do understand, Michael. Will you purchase the cloth? Will you put it here beneath this tree?'

He nodded.

'Do you need money to borrow a cart?' she asked suddenly.

His black eyes flashed. He turned away from her and, taking a pebble from the wall, he threw it hard at a distant rock. 'If I need money, Mistress Rosalie, I'll earn it,' he said with anger in his voice.

'I beg your pardon. I did not mean to offend you. I'll just get the money for the cloth.' She was about to leave when she stopped and turned. 'How does Michael Pendeen earn money?' she asked, suddenly intrigued.

'I'm a smuggler,' he said, keeping a solemn face with some difficulty, for his anger had gone as quickly as it came.

'Do you do nothing else?'

A broad smile spread over his bronzed face.

'I'm a sailor, a fisherman, I spend most of the time at sea.' Then he took a deep, slow breath and watched her face intently as he spoke. 'I'll soon have my own lugger. She's being built at Padstow. I'll show her to you whilst we're there.'

Rosalie made no attempt to hide her surprise. She came back to the wall eagerly. 'Your own lugger! How wonderful! What will you do with her?' She knew a lugger was a boat, but no more.

Michael sighed, then he leaned towards her and said softly, 'If you don't get the money, all the cloth'll be sold. There'll be time enough to talk of my boat on our journey. The sun's already well over the south-west.'

She left quickly without answering and was soon back with the money. 'Is this enough?' she asked.

'More than enough. I'll put what is left with the cloth. Forgive me for making you hurry, but I've other things to purchase in the market. I must also have sleep. I take a ship from Boscastle on the two o'clock tide.'

'You are smuggling tonight?' she asked anxiously, as he climbed the wall.

He shook his head. 'Not tonight. We've a cargo of slate from Delabole. Goodbye, Mistress Rosalie. I'll return,' he called.

When his lithe figure had been hidden by the branches, she heard a horse whinny, then hoofbeats on the bridle path. She made to return to the house, then stopped, rooted to the spot. I must be quite mad, she thought. Completely insane. I've said I'll go to Padstow. How the deuce will I explain my absence to Lucy and Robert? Her mind was in turmoil. Why did she want to go? Was it all a dream, this tall, dark-haired man who made her heart leap and pulse race. She tried desperately to tell herself it was not Michael himself, but the fact that he promised news of her brothers. The excuse eased her conscience for a time at least, but it was hardly convincing. She knew only that her growing friendship with him was exciting, even dangerous.

Robert returned from the town in a thoroughly bad mood, having achieved nothing. He told Rosalie of a particularly insolent young Cornishman he had encountered at the Bedford Arms who had suggested he dress as a smuggler and visit the coast by night. Robert brushed the dust off his riding jacket for the fourth time.

'Dashed handsome fellow he was, too,' he said thoughtfully. 'Taller than I, with black hair, and an emerald-green kerchief at his throat.'

Rosalie smothered a giggle.

'He even had the impudence to tell me where I could buy cloth for a disguise. Said something about a birch tree. Some ale house, I suppose.'

Rosalie got up from her chair and went to the window. She was unable to look at

Robert's face any longer. She would surely burst out laughing at any minute. Michael had really gone too far. He had no doubt presumed that Robert would recount the incident to her.

When Robert went up to change his riding clothes, she slipped out into the garden. Yes, there it was, under the silver birch where they had talked, a roll of blue Camelford woollen cloth and, on top, a wild rose of the palest pink.

Robert was surprised at Rosalie's industriousness during the next week. He had never known her to spend so much time with a needle. He did not enquire what she was making, which was just as well. He continued to get nowhere with his enquiries, as she had done. The October days were getting shorter; Robert returned for tea each day and remained in for the evening. Rosalie took pity on him after a few days. She told him that she had just received news that the boys were on a ship bound for America. She explained that she had promised not to reveal the source of her information.

He was surprised but pleased. 'Then I can take you home, Rosalie!' he exclaimed joyfully. 'We can leave on the stage tomorrow.'

She shook her head, much to Robert's dismay. 'Oh, no, Robert. I'll stay here. There may be more news. I shall stay until the boys return.'

Robert was deeply vexed; his face flushed scarlet, he paced the room angrily. 'This is ridiculous, Rosalie,' he said. 'Quite ridiculous. I insist that you return home.'

Lucy burst conveniently into the room, brandishing a letter that Robert had brought from the post house.

'It's from Hugh!' she cried, her soft grey eyes dancing with excitement. 'He says I'm to go to London in three days. Will you not come with me, dear Rosalie?'

Rosalie smiled, but shook her head. Robert had stopped pacing for a moment, a faint hope lifting his heart, but Rosalie dashed it again with one shake of her fair curls.

'I think not, Lucy,' she said, frowning now. She had forgotten that Lucy was hoping to join her husband for the winter in London. This upset her plans acutely.

Lucy acknowledged her refusal sadly, but smiled nevertheless. 'You're quite welcome to stay here in my absence, Rosalie,' she said.

Robert let out a deep sigh of despair. Lucy went on, in total ignorance of his suffering, 'You may use the house as your own. Indeed, it will keep the servants on their toes to have someone here. They become lazy when we are away. I swear the rooms are never cleaned during our absence. Anyway, I'll leave you to decide. I must go to plan my wardrobe. I can scarce believe I'm really to see London again.' She hurried away, with the excitement of a child who has been told of a birthday treat. Robert began pacing the room again, his hands clasped behind his back. He stared fixedly at the floor, with a quick glance up at Rosalie every now and then.

Rosalie took stock of the situation, her agile mind seeking a narrow shaft of daylight through the haze ahead. Suddenly she got to her feet and rushed over to Robert.

'Why, Robert,' she cried, taking his hands in hers and looking straight into his troubled eyes, 'I've a marvellous idea.'

He was so taken aback by her action, thrust off balance by the soft, warm touch of her hands in his, that he stood quite still, his heart racing, longing for her to say he could take her home.

Rosalie, a little out of breath, spoke quickly, eagerly. 'You can accompany Lucy to London, Robert. Then, as soon as the boys return, I'll follow. Then I can think clearly about your offer of marriage.' She kissed him impulsively on the cheek, hoping to sway him towards her way of thinking. Robert was confused. On the one hand, the statement that Rosalie intended to stay in Cornwall. Yet on the other, the mention of his proposal in a more favourable light. He did not know whether to be angry or pleased. He pressed her hands together between his and put them to his lips.

'Then I'll stay with you, Rosalie,' he declared vehemently.

Rosalie sighed. Only two days more to persuade Robert to leave. Once alone in her bedroom that evening, she wrote a hurried letter to Robert's mother.

When morning came, she was up early, requesting the groom to take it to the post house to catch the early northbound stage.

On the eve of Lucy's departure, Robert and Rosalie sat with her in the drawing-room at Trevia, talking and laughing. The large fireplace was ablaze with logs. They were glad of the warmth. The fields around were wrapped in a cold, grey mist. Lucy chatted gaily about her visit, but Rosalie knew that she was nervous of the journey. She would have been glad of Robert's company and protection. Rosalie waited patiently. She waited for the ideal moment when the ears of her companions were totally unoccupied, then she put on a startled, shocked expression, saying Robert's name in an equally shocked, startled voice.

Robert sprang to his feet with alarm. 'Rosalie! What the deuce is wrong?' he cried.

She stared at him with big blue appealing eyes. 'A chaperon,' she whispered huskily. 'I will not have a chaperon when Lucy is gone.'

Robert looked over to Lucy, then back to Rosalie. 'But I'll be here, Rosalie,' he said.

'That is it, Robert. That is it. You cannot stay alone with me, in the same house, without a chaperon. Oh, Robert, dear, what would your mother say?'

Robert saw the point. He frowned. He knew quite well what his mother would say. Then slowly a smile crept over his face. 'Mother does not know,' he announced. 'Surely you do not doubt my honour, Rosalie?'

Rosalie continued in a distressed voice, 'But it would be my honour, Robert. It would be in question, and indeed I fear your mother does know that Lucy is leaving Trevia. I happened to mention it in my last letter to her.'

Robert was stunned. 'Damnation, Rosalie! Did you not consider the position before imparting such news? I'll have to leave. It cannot be helped. If you will not come home with me, I cannot make you. You'll no doubt amuse yourself here until your brothers return, although it seems quite unnecessary to me.' He marched out of the room, flustered, and red in the face. 'I'll endeavour to pack. I trust it will not inconvenience you if I travel to London with you, Lucy?' He did not wait for an answer. He entered the hall and bounded up the stairs two at a time. Rosalie sighed a satisfied sigh and took up her sewing.

'You do not want him to stay, Rosalie.' Lucy wagged an accusing finger at her. 'You're mischievous. I cannot think why. The poor boy is so devoted to you. You treat him so badly.'

Rosalie put down her needle and regarded Lucy with anxiety. 'You will not tell him, Lucy? I do not want him hurt.'

Lucy shook her head. 'No. I'll not tell him. But there is more here that I could tell, if only I knew it.'

Rosalie sighed. 'I wish to be alone, to think more clearly. If I'm to make such a great decision as marriage, I must have a clear head. Robert should be far away from me, then I may observe how much I miss him. Then, when the boys return, I'll hurry home to give him my answer.'

Lucy frowned and nodded slowly. 'I see,' she said, but she was not convinced.

CHAPTER SIX

Rosalie walked impatiently backwards and forwards, putting the cloth bag that she carried down on the rough earth, then immediately picking it up again. She knew she was early. The time she had arranged to meet Michael had not yet arrived. She smoothed down the skirts of her new frock, the one she had made from the blue Camelford cloth. The material was rougher than those she was used to, but the simple style was one she had observed from the servants at Trevia. She put down the bag again, to pull a well-worn shawl further around her shoulders. A brown woollen cloak hung over her other arm.

The approaching sound of hooves reached her ears. She bit her lip with agitation. Then she told herself firmly she was being quite ridiculous, straightened her shoulders, took a deep breath and waited.

Michael reined the horse well before it reached her. He jumped down and came towards her with a smile.

'Will it do, Michael?' she asked anxiously, smoothing down her skirts again. 'Will my frock do justice to the part I play?'

He looked at her frock, then his eyes rested on her face, but he did not speak.

'Michael!' she cried impatiently. 'Is it not suitable?'

'You look like a queen to me,' he said with a laugh.

Rosalie sighed. 'Then it is no good. I cannot go.'

He lifted his hand to touch her shoulder, but dropped it immediately, remembering his place. 'Your frock, 'tis perfect, Mistress Rosalie,' he said. ''Tis you who look like a queen, whatever you wear.'

She gave a little nervous smile. 'Then you'll take me?'

''Twill be an honour, my lady,' he said. 'May I help you into your carriage?' He lifted her up on to the rough wooden seat of the cart. Rosalie was glad that there was at least a bar on which to rest her feet. She had seen many carts with none.

The light from the sun gave little warmth on this last day of October. Being raised above the shelter of the stone hedge, Rosalie felt the bitterness of the wind. She put on the cloak and wrapped it tightly around herself.

Michael took the reins lightly in his hands and the horse started forward. 'You're certain, Mistress Rosalie?' he asked quietly. 'Certain you wish to come with me? Look at the track, the ridges, the pot-holes. You've already felt the coldness of the wind. If you wish to return to Trevia, I'll take you.' He turned his head towards her, watching her face for any sign of regret. But her eyes remained steady and sure as she spoke.

'I'm quite certain, thank you. It will do me no harm to learn a little of the life of others. My brothers are surely doing this already.' She stopped speaking for a moment and watched a seagull as it wheeled above them, screeching its cry. It settled on a wall for a mere second before darting seawards. Rosalie sighed, then went on, 'I worry about their fitness for the task they have taken, Michael. They are used to study, not the labour of their hands.'

Michael smiled. 'Your worried thoughts'll not change their destiny,' he said. 'They just make you unhappy. Your brothers must accept the lot they've chosen. 'Twill do them no good if, when they return, their sister is become sick with worry for them.' He spoke sternly.

Rosalie acknowledged his wisdom with a smile.

'We'll drive on the turnpike a while,' he continued. ' 'Twill not be so pitted, though this cart, I fear, is no elegant coach.'

'Coaches have little comfort. They toss you about like the very devil,' Rosalie declared vehemently.

Michael smiled to himself. He wondered what Mr Robert James would say if he could see Rosalie now. No chaperon indeed. And who was her chaperon now? On a journey at the mercy of a Cornish smuggler. An honourable smuggler at least. Not that Michael Pendeen thought of himself as only a smuggler. A sailor, a fisherman. Smuggling was a bonus. The way he had managed to save enough money over the years to pay for the building of his own lugger. He did not intend to stay a peasant all his life. He'd buy other ships, a fast cutter, perhaps, then ... He sighed. Idle dreaming. Today he was a peasant, sitting in a cart beside a beautiful girl. Yet a girl so far above him that he couldn't even touch her shoulder without the self-inflicted pain of guilt.

Rosalie felt easier now, in mind if not in body. The wind was bitter on her cheeks, but the jolting of the cart was no more than she had expected. She was not a fool. She knew that although she was eager for news of her brothers' voyage, she had come today because she wanted to come. For the journey itself, the promise of excitement, of impending discovery. Most of all, perhaps, because she wanted to be with Michael Pendeen.

By noon, the turnpike was behind them, the

narrow twisting lane to St Teath ahead. Michael voiced his intention of stopping at the White Hart, where they could eat and drink.

'And what shall we drink?' Rosalie asked, knowing they had food in their bags.

Michael glanced at her with a wry smile. 'Will you take ale or brandy, Mistress Rosalie?' he asked.

She screwed up her face for a moment, considering. 'What would you recommend, Mr Pendeen?' she returned, undaunted.

He laughed. 'Perhaps a small tankard of cider'd be more to your liking. You'll not like ale, nor the spirits, I'll wager.'

'Then I shall have cider,' she announced. 'Is it not also time that you called me simply Rosalie, if I'm to be a plain Cornish maid?'

He laughed, shaking his head. 'That you'll never be. Neither Cornish nor plain. For, alas, Mistress Rosalie, you're too pretty to be plain and you speak too well to be Cornish.' He was silent for a moment, ducking his head to avoid a branch that hung low over the lane. 'I've with me,' he began, 'a distant cousin from the Midlands. She's been working in a big house—in service. She's clever with a needle—and had the good fortune to have a mistress who taught her to read. How does that sound, Mist—', he grinned, 'Rosalie?'

She laughed. 'I think that will suit me well.' She bent to pick up her bag. 'You've reminded me, I've a gift for you.' She took out a shirt and handed it to him. 'I did a little extra sewing when I made my frock. If it does not fit, you must tell me. I can alter it. I had to guess at your size.'

He took the shirt without speaking, halting the horse as he did so. It was made of fine silk. The sort that Robert would wear, embroidered on the yoke and cuffs. He ran his fingers gently over the material, then held it against himself. 'The shirt'll fit me well,' he said quietly, 'but will I ever fit such a shirt?'

'Do the clothes I wear today change the real me? If you wear a fine shirt, will you not still be Michael Pendeen? You said that you envied Robert his clothes. I thought it would please you.'

'Indeed it does. Perhaps more than you'll know. Not least 'cause you made it yourself. Thank you.' He folded it away and placed it carefully in his bag. 'We're almost at St Teath,' he said, flicking the reins. As they moved forward, he jumped down from the cart, leading the horse until he reached an inn, where he turned the cart into the yard.

Rosalie slowly sipped the cider that Michael brought her. A new taste, and bubbles that tingled in her mouth. Refreshing certainly, and—yes, she did like it. Michael had soon drunk his own ale and sat watching her with a look of secret amusement in his eyes.

A group of men laughed harshly together, sitting on the wooden benches outside the inn.

Michael had insisted she stay on the cart whilst he fetched the drinks. She sensed now that he was eager to get under way. Out of the corner of her eye, she saw two men moving unsteadily towards them, exuding raucous laughter as they came, raising their tankards as if toasting her. But their jeering was not friendly, nor their toast a compliment.

'Michael,' Rosalie began nervously, edging a little nearer to him on the seat.

'Give me your tankard,' he said calmly, keeping a watchful eye on the men. He took it from her quickly and put it with his own in the cart. 'Hold tight,' he breathed. He lifted the reins and struck the horse hard on the rear. The startled animal jerked forward so suddenly that the jeering men had to jump for their lives as the cart rolled towards them. At the side of the inn, Michael drove so close to the doorway that he had only to lean inside to return the tankards before taking the road again. They were followed for a time by a group of angry, shouting men.

'A little of the life of others,' Michael said wistfully. He glanced at Rosalie, saw her worried face, then laughed. 'Don't look so concerned, Rosalie,' he said. 'I've a fair reputation at wrestling, when I've a mind to fight.'

She managed a slight smile, sliding self-consciously back to her own part of the seat.

The cart rumbled on, past small farms and

cottages nestled in hollows against the wind. Past bare fields, their harvest reaped and ground. Over patchwork hills and down into autumn-hued valleys, where the stream ran fast, sparkling and loud.

The River Camel was running high when Michael first glimpsed its sandy estuary. The west wind had brought driving rain, beating against their faces like tiny knives. He had insisted that Rosalie sit behind him in the cart, for he had brought blankets for her, a thought for which she was deeply grateful as she sat huddled and sheltered in the corner. Michael turned the cart abruptly to the right, into the open gate of a grazing field. He flung the reins on to the seat, then, jumping down, he saw Rosalie and smiled. For despite the rough, wet ride she had fallen asleep.

He called her name, but she did not stir. He touched her shoulder gently. Her eyes flew open and she sat up, startled. 'We're at Rock,' he said. 'We leave the horse and cart here. I'll speak with the man at the cottage, then we'll cross the river.'

Rosalie nodded. She had slept little the night before, and felt better for her unexpected nap. Whilst Michael talked in the nearby stone cottage, she folded the blankets and climbed down. When Michael returned, he unhitched the horse, letting it free to graze in the field, then quickly picked up the blankets and his bag.

"'Tisn't far to the boat,' he said.

Rosalie's eyes widened in surprise. She had expected to cross the river by the bridge, but she did not admit to it.

They walked a short distance down the lane, then climbed over the sand dunes until they saw two small rowing-boats pulled up on to the beach. Rosalie looked at the river. It was the widest river she had ever seen. Wider even than the Trent. Such a great distance to the other side, and the boats looked so small. She climbed into one of them warily, taking the blankets from Michael and covering herself with one as he instructed.

'The tide's high,' he explained. 'The swell'll toss us about—' then he added, teasing her gently, 'like the very devil. The water'll break over the sides. Have no fear, Rosalie. We'll reach harbour safe.'

He heaved the boat down into the water, wading out until she was well afloat. Then he climbed in and took up the oars. The small boat was pitched and rolled as if it was made of paper. At times it seemed to almost stand on end. Rosalie was convinced that she must be thrown into the swirling water. She held on fervently, trusting Michael as he rowed up-river, then let the tide carry them back towards the entrance to Padstow harbour.

Michael's aunt, a tall, straight-backed woman, was both surprised and pleased to see her nephew. He was always welcome, and the maid he had brought, too. She eyed Rosalie carefully. The maid had a pretty face, but little to say. Michael explained that Rosalie was shy. She had to bite her mouth to prevent herself from giggling when he said this. She kept her eyes down, not daring to look into his.

The room she was given was small, but spotlessly clean. Its tiny windows overlooked the harbour, which delighted her. She found herself most conscious of her hands. When she was introduced to Michael's uncle and teenage cousins Emma and Clare, she wanted to hide them. Curious to feel ashamed of one's smooth, soft hands, she thought, but they had plainly never done any work. She was sure they would give her away.

Michael's uncle, Francis Tregar, was a shipping clerk. Not poor, but they had no servants. Emma Tregar, Michael's nineteen-year-old cousin, had from the first made Rosalie feel uncomfortable. She obviously considered that Michael was very much her own possession. His bringing Rosalie was not to her liking, although she retained a polite friendliness with her.

Michael seemed amused. He showed no particular desire to be alone with Emma, but he allowed her to wait on him, praised her cooking and even remarked how pretty she looked. All this in Rosalie's presence. Emma's younger sister, Clare, had no such notions as her sister. She was kind and helpful to Rosalie, a little shy of Michael.

Rosalie smiled to herself when Emma produced a kerchief she had made especially for him. When she gave it to him, he thanked her, then with a glint of boyish humour in his eye he fetched his bag. Rosalie watched Emma's face with interest.

'See, Aunt Harriet, what Rosalie made for me,' Michael said. Emma paled. She swung her dark curls, determined to show no interest. Mistress Tregar took the shirt in her hands and examined it closely.

'A fine shirt be that, Michael,' she said. 'Look you, Emma, you could learn some fine stitching from Rosalie. You'm too hasty. Too careless wi' yours.'

Rosalie looked up at Michael. When he met her gaze, she shook her head and frowned. Emma had gone off in a huff. Michael took Rosalie's hint, and followed Emma.

Mistress Tregar sat down beside Rosalie, still holding the shirt. ''Tis a beautiful silk, Rosalie,' she said. 'We canna' buy such cloth yere.'

Rosalie smiled. 'I bought it in Nottingham,' she said truthfully, but she did not tell her—nor would she tell Michael—that she had undone a newly made petticoat to make the shirt.

When Harry and John Tregar returned from fishing pilchards and found their cousin in Padstow, they wasted no time in deciding they were taking him out to 'The George' for an ale or two. Rosalie saw reluctance in Michael's eyes. He came over and sat down beside her on the sofa. He was silent for a while, just watching the firelight; then he spoke quietly so that only she could hear.

'Will you mind if I go out, Rosalie?' he asked.

'You surely do not have to ask me, Michael,' she said with a smile. 'I'm quite comfortable sitting here, thank you—and Emma is watching you very closely at this moment,' she added.

'Then I'll go,' he said softly. 'And Emma may do what the devil she pleases,' he added with a grin.

When the men had left, Rosalie was aware of a slight feeling of panic. When Mistress Tregar and her daughters took out their work-baskets, Rosalie gave a sigh of relief. Her offer to sew a hem was gladly accepted by Mistress Tregar; scowled at by Emma. Anticipating awkward questions, Rosalie made constant requests herself for information on life in Padstow. Her interest was appreciated, even Emma softened a little. They sewed until their eyes ached in the dim lamplight.

The men returned, talkative and noisy. Rosalie listened as John and Harry bragged about the haul they had taken that day on their boat. Michael was quieter, doing more listening than talking. He glanced across at

Rosalie at intervals, as if he wanted to ask if she had been all right in his absence.

Harry Tregar, twenty-four and overweight, appeared to have drunk in abundance. He walked unsteadily, needing the aid of the table for support.

'I hear you've been in service, young Rosalie,' Michael's uncle called loudly.

'Yes, I was,' she replied. 'Mostly in the sewing-room,' she added, forestalling questions she could not answer.

'Worked in a spinning mill for a time, did you not, Rosalie?' That was Michael. She felt like murdering him.

'Rough in the mill, is it?' John asked with interest. He was tall like Michael, with the same dark hair. 'What hours did 'ee work?'

Rosalie looked straight at Michael, her heart pounding. You get me out of that one, her eyes said. He took up the challenge with a grin.

'Thirteen hours a day, was it not, Rosalie? Locked in from morn till night.' He looked at his cousins as he spoke, avoiding Rosalie's scathing glance. 'Young children working the same as the mines, Rosalie told me.'

Rosalie scowled. She had told him no such thing. How did he know how long mill hours were, anyway? 'The children are quite well looked after,' she retorted angrily.

Harry Tregar, who had been watching her closely, came and sat down beside her now, almost falling on her in his effort to sit down.

He sprawled on the sofa and, throwing back his head, he laughed loudly. 'The devil they be,' he shouted. 'Mill 'n' mine owners, they'm all the same. Ride about in fine carriages, their ladies in they silk frocks. Their hands never soiled, whilst their workers starve.'

Rosalie felt herself grow pale, her bottom lip began to tremble. 'The children are well fed and clothed,' she insisted. 'They have houses specially built for them, and medical care when they're sick.' She longed to say: At least, that is so in my mill. Then she heard Michael speak again.

'I've a notion,' he said slowly, 'there's mills where the workers are well treated. There's some who's good masters.' He did not add: good mistresses.

Harry laughed in scorn. 'A likely tale! They eat the cream and leave only sour milk for the workers. Two bairns dead in Wheal Jane a-Tuesday, choked o' the dust, did 'ee. What do ee die of in mills, Rosalie?' He flung his arm across the sofa behind her, pushing his red face near to hers.

Michael's voice came loud and demanding, 'Leave her alone, Harry. 'Tis a wearying journey we had. I've a mind to be in bed soon. I think Rosalie's tired, too. Is there a bite to eat, Aunt Harriet?'

His aunt got to her feet. 'There's bread and cheese, and tea if you want it, though I think you men've quenched your thirst enough tonight.' She took a candle and bustled off into the kitchen. Rosalie stood up quickly and followed. She was glad to rid herself of the closeness of Harry Tregar.

Rosalie carried the cheese dish into the sitting-room. She was unsure whether she should ask for a tablecloth. No one suggested it, so she put the dish down on the bare wooden table. Michael had disappeared. She could hear Clare and Emma giggling outside on the quay, so she guessed he was with them. She brought in the loaf she was given, cups, saucers, and, in fact, Rosalie set the whole table. She was feeling quite pleased with herself when Mistress Tregar came in with a pot of tea.

'You've forgot the breadboard, m'dear. 'Tis over the dresser.'

Rosalie took a candle. She went back down the long passage into the kitchen. She held it up and walked slowly around the kitchen, shielding the wavering light against the draught with her hand. A breadboard? What did a breadboard look like? The bread at her home was cut in the kitchen and served on china plates. She found the dresser and inspected its shelves. Then she heard footsteps behind her on the flagstones.

Thinking it to be Mistress Tregar, she put out her hand and took a small wooden board from the shelves quickly. That must be it.

A strong arm encircled her waist. Michael? How dare he! The colour rushed to her cheeks.

Then the smell of stale alcohol blasted in her face as Harry Tregar pressed his cheek close to hers and whispered slurringly in her ear.

'I've a liking for a spirited wench,' he breathed. 'Aye, an' a fair pretty one at that.' She tried to move away from him, indignant, angry, but he spun her round to face him and pressed his hot lips hard against hers. She struggled and writhed, but his arms held her in an iron grip. Why does someone not come? she thought frantically. When he lifted his face from hers, he threw back his head and laughed.

'Little bundle o' fire, you be. I like that.'

Rosalie exploded. 'How dare you, sir!' she shouted. 'Unhand me at once!'

For a moment Harry Tregar looked shocked, the authority in her voice made him stare. Then his arms tightened around her, bending her body backwards with his own. The candlelight flickered across his red, puffy face, and Rosalie saw his leering smile and excited, bloodshot eyes.

Rosalie swung the breadboard. Harry Tregar stood for a moment with blank eyes, then his arms fell from her waist. He slipped limply to the floor and lay in a heap on the flagstones.

Rosalie stared. The pale glow of the candle hardly reached the dark mass at her feet. 'I've killed him!' she gasped, her heart thumping loud and fast. 'Oh, God! What shall I do?' She felt the colour drain slowly from her cheeks.

She pulled her foot out from underneath Harry Tregar, then she ran, down the passage, out of the front door.

Michael was alone when she saw him. He leaned on the harbour wall, staring out over the dark river. She tugged at his arm before he saw her, pulling him round, her breath hot, choking and fast, her heart still pounding.

'Rosalie!' he exclaimed with surprise. Then, sensing her distress in the darkness, he took her firmly by the shoulders.

'What's amiss?' he demanded. Had there been a light to see she would have seen his face grow tense with anger. 'Is it Harry?' he said.

She tried to speak, but her voice would not come. He pulled her to him and smoothed her hair with a gentle hand until she stopped trembling.

'I've killed him, Michael,' she whispered at last.

'You've done what?'

A cold chill ran through her body. She shuddered the next few words. 'I've—k-killed him. He k-kissed m-me. I hit him w-with the b-breadboard.' She swallowed hard. 'He's on the f-floor in the k-kitchen.'

Michael did not speak. He took off his jacket and put it round her shoulders, then he took her firmly by the hand and led her back into the kitchen. Harry Tregar still lay on the floor. Michael told Rosalie to stay by the door, then he took the candle from the dresser and knelt down. Rosalie stood waiting, still shivering.

'He's not dead, Rosalie. You've stunned him. He's more drunk than anything,' he said at last. 'He deserves to be dead. I'll fetch John. We'll take him up to his bed.' He came over to Rosalie, lifting the candle so that he could see her face clearly. 'He'll not touch you again. I'll vow that. I'll deal with Harry Tregar in the morning when he's sober. You're not hurt?' he asked anxiously.

She shook her head.

'I apologise, Rosalie, for the behaviour of a man who's my cousin, that I allowed you to be alone with him. Do you want supper?' he asked, opening the door.

'No, thank you. I could not eat now.' She had stopped shivering, feeling only relief.

'If you'll go to your room, I'll send Clare up with a warm drink. I'll explain to my aunt. Her door's across from yours if you need anything.'

Rosalie nodded. 'Good night, Michael. Thank you.' She took off his coat and handed it to him.

He smiled slightly, heaving a deep sigh. 'Thank you for what?' he said. 'For allowing you to be insulted?' He gave her the candle. She saw that his anger had not gone. 'Good night, Rosalie,' he called as he walked quickly towards the living-room door.

When she reached her own room she bolted the door behind her. The lives of the others, she thought sadly. Peter and Ben were with men like Harry Tregar. She sighed. They were still so young, so impressionable, but surely the good manners they had been taught would not leave them. Yet to these men of Cornwall, they too were already men; not the children she thought them to be. Would they be drinking strong liquor, swearing, and insulting women, when they returned? The disgust came back to her. She flung off her clothes angrily. Then she thought of Michael. All men are not so, she mused. Michael drank, she had heard him swear, but he had honour and good manners. There must be other Cornish men like him. They could not all be such animals as Harry Tregar.

CHAPTER SEVEN

Sitting on the steps by the harbour wall was uncomfortable and bitingly cold. A storm was blowing from the sea, howling and moaning round the chimney pots, upturning lobster baskets in its swirling path. Rosalie sat waiting, watching the seagulls sheltering in the lee of the harbour. Some resting on the weed-dragging ropes. Some gleaning between the slats of empty fish boxes for the scraps of wasted pilchard or mackerel. The bare sand of the low tide held few boats. The fishing craft, far out at sea, must wait for a full harbour again before they could seek refuge from the gale.

Michael had gone to see the owner of the *Padstow Mermaid*. He had been gone half an hour already. Rosalie was getting more than just a bit impatient. She got to her feet, her eyes scanning the quay for a hurrying figure, but none came. The hood of her cloak was thrust suddenly from her head, her long, fair hair flew over her face. She pushed it back and pulled up the hood with annoyance as she sat down again to gain the shelter of the wall.

Why did he not come? He had no right to keep her waiting so long. She sighed. No right. Was it not she who had no right? She was here at her own invitation. Was it not Michael who was doing her a favour by the enquiries he had been making? She resigned herself to wait more patiently, or at least to try.

Two fishermen sat only a short distance away. Their wrinkled old hands worked steadily as they mended the nets of the younger men. They seemed not to notice the wind, totally ignoring its gusts. Like Michael, she thought. He rarely appeared to even feel the wind, as though he was so used to its beating against his face that he counted it a friend.

A young woman hurried past with a small boy clinging to her skirts. She climbed the stone steps of a tall building near by and vanished inside. Rosalie watched the child, then tears filled her eyes as she remembered Ben. Ben clinging to her skirts when she was thirteen or fourteen, begging her to play with him when she wanted to go riding with Robert. She brushed away the tears and lifted her head. The joyous possibility of knowing how long it would be before she saw her brothers again had tormented her from the moment she had woken.

She had come downstairs warily, feeling some want of courage for a meeting with Harry Tregar. Thankfully, John and he had already left, a fact given to her pointedly by Mistress Tregar as soon as she entered the kitchen, then added to with a knowing look at Michael.

'I think my younger son will be feeling more than a little the worse for last night. Michael escorted him down to the boat.'

Rosalie could smile now at her prowess with the breadboard. Nothing seemed so bad in the light of day.

A familiar voice broke her thoughts as Michael sat on the steps at her side. She turned to him eagerly. From his smiling face she deduced the news was good.

'They're on the *Padstow Mermaid*,' he said. 'They gave their names as Peter Lewis and Ben Hawkey, but I'm sure 'tis them.'

Rosalie put an impatient hand on his arm. 'When are they returning? When shall I see them?' she asked.

Michael laughed. 'The ship won't sail straight for England, Rosalie. She'll go to Spain from America, then return to Cornwall.'

Rosalie's face fell. 'But that will take much longer,' she cried.

'A little,' he said. 'I've calculated that she may put in at Padstow by the middle of June, but don't hold me to it. 'Tis not that long to June,' he said, with almost sadness in his voice.

Rosalie stood up, lifted her eyes to the sky, gave a deep sigh, then she looked down at him and smiled. 'Oh, Michael,' she said, 'I'm so happy to have real news of them at last. I do not think I completely believed you before. I've had such fears that I'd never see them again.'

Michael got slowly to his feet, his face grave for a moment.

'I wish you to be happy, Rosalie,' he said slowly. 'But they're not safe home yet. There's three thousand miles of fickle, treacherous sea between here and America. There's no surety in crossing the sea, but I pray God'll be merciful and deliver them safe.'

When he saw the change in her face, as the joyous light burned low in her eyes, he gave a gesture of regret, then he smiled. 'The news is still good. We're at least sure where they are.' He lifted her chin with the crook of his finger. 'Will you come and see my boat? Or are you too cold?'

She shook her head. 'I'm not too cold,' she said, ably disguising the fact that she was.

They walked the length of the quay, reaching at last a large boatyard. Michael led the way inside, his eagerness alive on his face. He did not hesitate, passing without a glance the other boats in their various stages of construction. His lugger stood high on her blocks, the bare hull seeming to Rosalie raw, unprotected against the weather.

'Is she not beautiful, Rosalie?' he asked, his black eyes shining with pride. 'She's cost me many a night's sleep and years of hard work, but is she not worth it?'

Rosalie could not tell him that the boat looked the same as the others to her, just a plain wooden boat. She knew that Michael saw her with her masts raised, sails billowing in the wind. Perhaps most of all he saw his own name painted on the bows.

'She is indeed beautiful, Michael,' she said. 'What will you call her?'

He did not answer, but walked right around the boat, coming towards Rosalie from the other side.

'I've not decided,' he said. 'There's time enough for a name.'

When they returned to the Tregars' house, Michael's aunt was waiting for him with a message.

'Aaron Martin's been asking for 'ee, Michael,' she said. 'Captain Pengelly's sick. He wants you to take out the *Pencarrow* tonight. She's a cargo of tin for Ireland. He's mighty glad to find you'm in Padstow. Rosalie's welcome to stay wi' us while you'm gone.'

Michael furrowed his brow for a moment,

then glanced at Rosalie. ''Tis an offer I can't refuse,' he said. 'I'd best go and tell him so right away.' He opened the front door and was gone.

Rosalie fumed inside. She did not speak, but stormed angrily up to her room. She threw off her cloak, then put it on again because it was cold. Confound it! she thought. Why did these people not light the fires in their bedrooms? She sat on the bed and wrung her hands together with indignation. How dare he? How dare he assume she would not mind staying longer. He had not even asked her. She banged her hand down on the bed with anger. Well, she would not stay! He could take her back to Trevia this very day. She would tell him as soon as he returned. She watched from her window, then she saw him enter the harbour and hurried out to meet him on neutral ground.

He saw her coming towards him and waited. She had a scowl on her face and by the determination of her walk he knew what to expect.

'I wish to return to Trevia today,' she announced, standing as high as she could, though looking down on Michael was hardly a practical possibility.

Michael did not answer straight away; he just stood looking straight into her eyes.

Rosalie took a deep breath, preparing to repeat her announcement. Then she stopped. Was it her imagination, or was there a flicker of humour in his eyes? He was laughing at her.

How dare he? The colour rushed to her cheeks. It was so intolerable that she had always to look up at him.

''Twill not be possible for you to return today,' he said, catching her off balance. 'Unless you wish to swim the river and walk home.' His mouth gave a slight twitch as if he were trying hard not to laugh. 'I've accepted the job. I'll not go back on my word.'

Rosalie opened her mouth, then shut it again. She stamped her foot, took another deep breath, then began, 'You will take—'

'You're not dressed for such behaviour, Rosalie,' he reminded her. 'Aye, and the eyes of Padstow's on you.'

She glanced down at her frock, then quickly around her. The groups of people who had been talking together were watching her with interest, her voice raised in anger attracting their attention. She knew what he meant and she was furious. She turned on her heel and went straight back to the house.

She did not speak to Michael when he followed her in, or even later when he came down to tea after having a sleep in his room in preparation for sailing on the midnight tide. Mistress Tregar invited Rosalie to accompany them to hear John Wesley that night and Rosalie mellowed a little. She was intrigued to hear this man of whom she had heard so much. She walked sedately beside Mistress Tregar, ignoring Michael completely. He walked with

Emma, who chatted away to him continuously. They make a good couple, Rosalie thought.

When they arrived at the open-air meeting place, few people were there yet. Michael and Emma headed straight for the brown wall of a building and leaned on it. When Clare and Mistress Tregar had also leaned themselves on the wall, Rosalie found herself next to Michael, which displeased her greatly. She stood erect with dignity. She had been taught to hold herself upright, not to lean on any available prop.

The crowds were gathering. John Wesley stood on a wooden platform and began with a prayer. Whilst the opening hymn was being sung Rosalie found herself listening to Michael. He had quite a remarkable voice. Then his singing stopped suddenly and she sensed him leaning towards her.

'If you'll lean on the wall, Rosalie, you'll find 'tis warm,' he said in a low voice.

Rosalie ignored him. Then her curiosity got the better of her; she put one hand behind her so that Michael could not see and felt the wall. To her surprise, it was indeed warm. In fact, it was hot. She edged her feet very slowly back until her heels touched it, allowing her to stand erect, not appearing to lean, yet to feel the warmth through her whole body. She could not imagine how the wall of a house could get so comfortably hot.

Michael stopped singing again and bent to whisper in her ear. ''Tis the bakehouse,' he said, as if reading her thoughts.

John Wesley preached about the evil of drink. When he spoke of smuggling, the feet of the congregation seemed to shuffle in unison. Rosalie could not resist glancing up at Michael to see if he was really listening. He was staring up at the sky, the gaunt angles of his young face lit well by a nearby lamp.

Can smuggling be so wrong? Rosalie thought, her anger with him fading rapidly. Is it truly fair that these people should be so poor without it, yet the men in London who gleaned their taxes grow fat of excess? She knew Michael feared God. But what did he pray? For forgiveness, from smuggling, when he knew he would do it again the next night?

John Wesley was coming to the end of his sermon. Michael looked quickly down from the sky straight into Rosalie's questioning eyes. She turned her head away with embarrassment. The final hymn was being sung. What do I know of sin? she thought. I have never been hungry enough to steal. Then she remembered the mill children, the people who worked for her, the fact that she had had no idea what hours they worked. Was it not as much a sin to do too little, as to do wrong? John Wesley's message disturbed her.

When the meeting ended, she walked silently back towards the quay. She did not notice that

Mistress Tregar and her daughters had walked the other way to call on friends. Only Michael walked beside her, in silence. When she noticed him there he asked, 'Am I allowed to walk with you, or must I walk behind?'

She stopped and turned towards him. 'Michael,' she said, her voice unsteady, 'I'm sorry.' The wind caught her cloak and she shivered. He took off his greatcoat and put it around her shoulders, gently lifting out her long hair.

'We're both to blame, Rosalie,' he said softly. 'But I must work to earn my living.' He sighed. 'I'm glad we're friends before I sail. I'd not like to be at sea with you angry with me.'

The four days at Padstow passed pleasantly enough whilst Michael was away. Rosalie helped a little around the house, her observant mind recording all the time. Noting the way that dusting was done, dishes were washed, things she had never concerned herself with before. As a guest, she was expected to do a little, her help with the mending and dressmaking was considered a great boon by her hostess.

It was the weather that caused most concern in the Tregar household. John and Harry were still away at sea. By the time Michael was due to return, the gales had worsened. Spring tides were mentioned, but Rosalie did not know what they meant; it was almost winter. She went to bed on the Saturday night with

Mistress Tregar's words still in her ears. 'If any man can bring that boat in safe, 'tis Michael,' she had said.

It was eleven o'clock when Michael's aunt knocked lightly on Rosalie's door. 'The *Pencarrow*'s safe in harbour,' she said. 'Michael'll soon be in his bed.'

Rosalie thanked her, then turned over and slept more soundly. She was awakened barely two hours later by a loud banging on her door. She lit the candle hurriedly, throwing her brown cloak around her shoulders. The curtains at the small window were swinging in the wind, water splashing seemed louder than usual. The window was shut tight. She heard voices shouting on the quay. Boats creaked at their moorings, then splintering wood. Footsteps running up the stairs. The rain was beating hard against the glass, resounding like a drum.

The banging began on her door again, muffled by the howl of the wind as it roared from the sea. She drew back the bolt quickly, then gasped in surprise.

Michael stepped into her room, ducking his head under the beam. He was still fully dressed. The flame of the candle in his hand bowed sideways, flared up brightly, then was extinguished abruptly by the cold draught. His face was tired and anxious.

''Tis the river, Rosalie,' he explained. ''Tis in flood; there's only an inch or two downstairs, but the tide's not turned yet.'

He saw the look of horror spring into her eyes. 'We're not in danger,' he said firmly. 'But we must be ready. Have you looked from your window?'

She shook her head. 'I've only just woken.'

He smiled at her. 'You do well to sleep on such a night.' He crossed to her window, where, bending low, he pulled back the curtain. 'See, we're all on ships,' he said with a short laugh. Rosalie joined him. She shivered at the cold draught that came in through the cracks in the woodwork. Then she stared with astonishment, for the water she had heard splashing was not in the harbour, but swilling across the quay. Small boats wrenched from their moorings were being thrown mercilessly against the house walls. They splintered like dry twigs against the granite. The water swirled, filling every gap it could find, carrying in its wake the nets and lobster baskets that had been left ready for the morning's fishing. Candles flickered in the windows of almost every building. White faces peered out. The *Pencarrow*, which Michael had moored only an hour before, strained at her ropes, her tall masts rising higher every second as the tide came on, neither heeding nor caring that there was no room for it.

Rosalie straightened her back from bending to the low window. Her face was white, her brain numbed by what she saw. She looked up at Michael, her hand gripping his arm. Then, as her eyes met his, the sound of the wind ceased. The noise-filled world around them vanished. She had felt the cloak fall apart as she had turned and put out her hand, yet suddenly she did not care. She did not care that this young Cornishman saw her in only the soft folds of her silk nightgown. A fierce fluttering filled her inside. She felt a strange compulsion to move nearer to him.

As he stood looking down at her, his dark eyes betrayed the same strong desire. He stood unmoving, struggling against his own emotions, his eyes saying everything that was in his heart.

Heavy footsteps passed outside the door. The world flooded back. Michael sighed, almost breathing relief that the thread was broken. He took the soft hand that still gripped his arm and pressed it hard.

'Trust me!' he said hoarsely. 'We'll keep watch till the tide turns. If there's danger, I'll come for you. Dress yourself ready, then go back to bed.' He smiled, stifling a yawn. 'I fear we'll be noisy a while yet. We're bringing the furniture upstairs for safety.'

'Michael!—Where's Michael?' Emma's irritated voice came to them.

'He's talking to Rosalie. Go back to bed,' her father's voice scolded.

'Oh!' A knock on the door told them that Emma had not gone back to bed.

Rosalie pulled the cloak together hurriedly, her cheeks flushed, her heart racing. She glanced up at Michael; for a fleeting second the same compelling force passed between them.

'Come in, Emma,' she said, the calmness in her voice a great effort. Her heart added, 'You may take him with you if you wish, but he's not yours—he's mine—if I want him.'

Emma's face peered round the door. She flashed a suspicious look at Rosalie, then took Michael's arm. 'My workbasket, Michael,' she said, 'and a wooden box of my things in the dresser, I must have they upstairs. You'll fetch they, won't 'ee?' she pleaded.

Michael lit his own candle again with the one that stood on Rosalie's washstand. He followed Emma to the door, but before he left he turned back towards Rosalie and smiled. 'Trust me?' he whispered.

'I do,' she said, returning the smile. 'Completely.'

When the door had closed, she sat down on the bed slowly. She did not hear the wind or feel the cold. Her body was warmed by a burning glow. Her cheeks on fire. How glad she was that Michael was back. She lay down on the bed and stared up at the flickering ceiling. Why had she never felt like this before? She had looked into Robert's eyes so many times, but never had there been the magnetic power she had just experienced.

Suddenly she sat up, flung off her cloak and

started to dress. Why did she always have to think of Robert? To compare. Was Robert her conscience? She did not need to be told this friendship was wrong, even dangerous. She knew full well that it was. Yet she had no intention of ending it, not at the moment at least. The floor felt suddenly cold to her bare feet. She glanced quickly out of the window, then lay on the bed under the quilt.

The long hours till morning dragged for Rosalie. When she had put out the candle, the blackness of the room seemed oppressive, frightening. She had lit it again, as she lay listening to the noisy night.

Dawn had come almost unnoticed, the dark, fast-riding clouds letting through little more light than the full moon had given.

When Rosalie opened her door, Michael was climbing the stairs. His face held the signs of intense weariness, his eyes were heavy, his clothes soaked from his boots to his shirt. Rosalie heard his aunt talking to Clare in the next room. She took one look at Michael, flung open her door, and pulled him inside. Then, closing the door quickly, she picked up a chair and set it beside him. He sank gratefully down on to it, his arms falling limply on to his lap, his head falling back on to the high rail.

His eyes closed for a moment of sheer exhaustion. 'Thank you,' he said simply.

Rosalie sat on the bed. She looked worriedly at his wet clothes, but avoided his eyes when he lifted his head.

'I've—' he began, sensing she was waiting for an explanation. 'I've been helping the neighbours with their furniture,' he said. 'Then we've been getting sand.' He stopped for a moment, wiped his forehead with the back of his hand. Then he went on, 'We'll put sacks of sand at the doors when the tide comes in again.'

'Are you going to bed now?' she asked.

'Not just yet. I wish to talk to you.' He shivered, feeling the wetness of his clothes now that he was sitting.

'Go and change first,' she said. 'I'll wait.'

'I've a mind to tell my aunt who you are,' he said, ignoring her order.

Rosalie sprang to her feet in surprise. 'Why?' she demanded.

'My aunt,' he said, keeping a low voice, 'and my cousins'll soon be cleaning the house, now the water's down. You cannot do this, so I'll tell her.'

'You will do no such thing,' she retorted angrily.

Michael sighed. He had not much strength left to argue. He saw Rosalie was spoiling for a fight. 'You don't understand,' he whispered. 'The job's dirty. I'll not allow you to do it.'

'But you will allow Emma to do it.'

'She's used to such things. It's happened before,' he said with a shrug.

'You think I am not as capable as Emma!'

Rosalie's voice was getting louder, giving Michael cause for concern. He had entered her room on the first occasion with the full knowledge of his uncle, persuading him that Rosalie would be less startled if it was he who explained to her about the flooding, but a second time he had no excuse.

'Please keep your voice down, Rosalie,' he whispered.

Rosalie sat down on the bed with exasperation. 'Well?' she whispered. 'Answer my question.'

He sighed and leaned towards her. ''Tis not a case of being capable,' he said, almost angrily. 'You're not to be allowed to do it. I'll bring you some books till we're finished.'

'You sound like Robert,' she said sulkily.

Michael grinned. 'I don't look like Robert,' he said, glancing down at his wet clothes.

'No,' she replied, completely without thinking. 'You are much taller and darker, and Robert is too—' She stopped, realising with embarrassment what she was saying. The colour rushed to her cheeks, she turned away from him to the window. Michael raised his eyebrows, but did not comment.

The water had fallen back into the harbour, but it had left behind the debris and mud.

'You see,' Michael said slowly, 'what a task cleaning up'll be.'

'I will borrow a frock from—'

'From Emma?' Michael shook his head. 'If I

wasn't so tired I'd put you over my knee,' he said.

'You would not dare,' she said, her whisper getting louder again.

Michael's black eyes flashed and he went to the door, his weariness forgotten for a moment. 'We shall see,' he said with a grin.

In a very short time he was back, changed and dry. Rosalie kept her distance from him. She had decided in his absence that he would dare if he chose, so she was wary.

'Will you let me tell my aunt?' he enquired hopefully.

'If you tell her now,' she said, 'she'll know that you lied to her. I'll not have her think badly of you for my sake.'

Clare's voice came to them as she passed the door, then Emma's asking for Michael. Rosalie went to the door and, realising she was going to open it, Michael got behind it quickly.

'Good morning,' she said brightly. 'If one of you ladies could lend me an old frock, I'll come down to help you.'

Emma said nothing. Clare looked expectantly at her mother for advice; she was painfully aware of her thinness.

'Of course, m'dear,' Mistress Tregar said warmly. 'Emma, get one of your frocks for Rosalie.'

Emma opened her mouth as if to speak.

'At once!' her mother commanded.

Michael stifled a laugh behind the door.

Rosalie took the frock that Emma brought and thanked her. She kept her foot against the door, forestalling any effort on Emma's part to see into the room. When Emma's footsteps had reached the lower stairs, Michael spoke.

'I'll say no more,' he said. 'You're determined.'

He left the room quickly and went down the stairs himself. When Rosalie saw the high-tide mark on the mud-soaked walls, smelt the pungent odour that the sea had left, she stood motionless and stared. Her hand touched the wet, slimy surface; she shuddered involuntarily.

'What the deuce am I doing?' she asked herself ruefully. 'I have servants who do this sort of thing.' She turned quickly and climbed up the stairs before she had been seen. As her hand touched the door-handle of her room, she heard voices in the kitchen below. Michael, telling his aunt that he could sleep later, as she tried to persuade him to go up to bed.

Rosalie froze where she was, her pride taking over. She knew he was staying downstairs because he thought she would need his help. She returned down the stairs and let herself quietly into the kitchen. Mistress Tregar was heating water over the fire. Emma and Clare were already washing down in the living-room.

Michael stood with his back to her. He leaned heavily on a wooden chair, the only one left in the room. Rosalie came up silently behind him. She dug a finger in his ribs as if it were a pistol and whispered in his ear.

'Bed, Mr Pendeen,' she said. 'This instant.'

He turned round slowly to look at her. He had half-expected her to faint at the sight, let alone actually do any work. He could hardly stand. His body ached with the weariness of nights without sleep on the stormy Celtic sea, then tonight, when he thought at least he would spend it in bed, he had hauled sand and moved furniture for most of the night. Yet he had to wait, to see if Rosalie would really want to tackle such a dirty job. As she looked at him now, her eyes were laughing. He knew she would be equal to the task.

'Aunt Harriet,' he said, not taking his eyes from Rosalie's face, 'I'll go up to my bed now. Rosalie's come to help you.'

CHAPTER EIGHT

Rosalie turned over in her bed in the warm bedroom at Trevia. She pulled the covers well over her head to muffle the sound of the rain beating on the window pane. But the sound persisted, a clattering sound. She listened, her eyes wide open, her heart pounding. That was not rain. It was as if something was falling from the roof on to the pane. Birds—It must be birds in the eaves. She thumped her pillow, turned it over and flung herself down on to it. Clatter—clatter, clatter—clatter. The sound went on.

Rosalie sat up in bed, swung her bare feet out on to the floor, then marched to the window. Something hit the glass as she reached it. She eased back the curtain gently, peering cautiously out. Then her nervousness vanished. The tense lines on her face melted into a smile, for there in the moonlight, poised in readiness to throw another pebble, was Michael Pendeen.

She had met him several times since he had returned her safely to Trevia. One Saturday he had taken her to a fair at St Teath. She had watched him wrestle, terrified he would get hurt, until he had returned to her triumphant, with the silver buckle he had won. Many times during the weeks that had passed, she had made plans to return to Nottingham. She told herself continually that she was being unkind to him, even cruel. She was the golden apple at the top of the tree that he could never have, yet she stayed.

Lucy Trevia had written to say that she and Hugh were going to Europe for the winter. Hugh, she said, had been pleased that Rosalie was staying at Trevia and had sent his assurance that Rosalie was welcome to stay as long as she wished.

When Michael was away at sea for days on end Rosalie had worried about his safety, vowing to leave as soon as he returned. Then, suddenly, he was back, with a promise of a visit to a donkey derby at Port Isaac, a picnic on the beach at Bossiney. Back, also, the excitement, the strong compulsion she had to be by his side. The hours they spent together were gay, full of laughter. There were times when she thought how much he reminded her of Peter. Perhaps it was her brothers with their reckless ways she missed. Then she would sigh. Michael was no boy, reckless at times maybe, but he was a full ten years older than Peter. She knew only too well that his thoughts of her were not those of a brother.

When Michael saw the window open, he dropped the pebbles in his hand and springing lightly on to his horse he rode under the window.

She leaned down towards him. 'Do you never sleep at night, Michael Pendeen?' she whispered.

His eyes laughed up at her. 'There's a ship wrecked at Trebarwith, Rosalie. Are you coming?'

Her eyes opened wide. 'Now?'

'Aye, now. Are you coming? You can ride up with me.' She nodded quickly, her eyes sparkling with excited anticipation.

When the window closed, Michael led his horse into the shadows. Only ten minutes later, Rosalie crept round the corner of the house, dressed in her 'Camelford' frock. She did not see Michael, but she heard his horse snort, then sensed he was beside her. He did not speak, but lifted her up on to the horse, then swung himself up in front of her. The moonlight came and went, as a fierce westerly pushed the heavy clouds across the night sky. Rosalie clasped her arms tightly round Michael's waist as they rode, glad of the shelter of his body from the cold blast.

'What kind of ship is wrecked?' she shouted in Michael's ear.

'An East Indiaman,' he called back, his voice carrying more easily than hers.

'Michael!' Rosalie's body stiffened suddenly, a terrifying doubt alarming her brain.

The horse slowed its pace as he heard her cry and tightened the rein. He turned his head, puzzled, anxious.

'The ship,' she stammered. 'It was not wrecked on purpose?' She felt him sigh as the horse came to a halt. He turned half-round to face her, a flicker of amusement in his eyes.

'Rosalie,' he said, 'ships are rarely wrecked that way these days. Mr Wesley was very persuasive when he preached the wickedness of such actions.' As the moon crossed her face he saw a questioning still in her eyes. He smiled. 'I've never in all my life taken part in the wrecking of a ship. Except the revenue boats, of course.'

'And they do not count?'

'Nay, Rosalie, they don't count.' He turned back and kicked the horse into motion again.

As they neared the coast, they came upon others heading in the same direction, some walking, some riding, both men and women, most carrying axes and sacks in their arms.

Michael took the cliff path from Trebarwith village, and they rode through a narrow gorge. Coming out of it, Rosalie saw in the distance a silver light, stretching from the moon like a shimmering pathway. A pathway that told her it crossed the sea.

The horse began descending between high brambles, nettles and bracken. At times, the rough path dropped suddenly, but Michael's pony never stumbled, seeming to know his way, slowing his pace or trotting on, needing no guidance from his master.

Rounding a sudden curve, Rosalie gasped as the land dropped away from them, sheer down into the valley. The horse trod carefully, keeping close to the cliff wall, and suddenly the roar of the sea reached their ears, echoing across the valley. The flapping of wings, which had at first startled Rosalie, now became a regular occurrence as the curlews left their nests, disturbed by the passing horse.

The ocean's roar grew gradually louder. Michael reined the horse, then dismounted. 'We'll walk from here,' he said. 'The path gets steeper.' He lifted Rosalie down beside him, taking her hand. They walked on, the large patches of slate in the path dropping acutely for a time. Then Michael stopped.

'I'll tether the pony,' he said, leading him up a slope to a well-used post.

When they continued, the path zig-zagged down to the cove. Rosalie was glad of Michael's steady hand. She wondered how many times before he had come that way in the night. A dark cloud plunged them abruptly into complete blackness. Still Michael walked on, crossing the well-worn slate that led to the beach with complete confidence. When the moon threw down its light again she saw they were just leaving a narrow channel cut out of the rocks, to come in full view of the beach.

Rosalie stopped walking and just stared. The long beach, exposed by a low tide, was crowded with people. Horses stood waiting, loaded with heavy packs on either side. Carts piled high with anything their owners could find. The frothing sea was choked with debris. Floating shadows on the water, spotlighted for seconds at a time whenever the moon appeared. Bales of cotton beside broken timber. Sacks of rice, swollen by the salt water, and wet slimy hides.

A man beside them started to fight with his neighbour over piles of clothes taken from a dead sailor. Michael pulled Rosalie nearer to his side.

'You'll stay close to me,' he said. 'We're in rough company. You'll not leave my side.' He spoke it as an order, but she knew she would obey him. He guided her from the beach on to a flat expanse of rock.

'Are you not going to load your horse with these cargoes from the Indian continent?' she said.

Michael shook his head. 'My horse's enough to carry with its extra load from Trevia. Tonight we'll watch.'

People were arguing, snatching wood from each other, although the sea was still filled with plenty more. They waded into the water, shouting joyfully at each valuable find, then carrying it ashore they pushed it furtively into their waiting sacks.

As Michael and Rosalie stood watching, a group of men staggered drunkenly towards them, cursing the treacherous sea, yet their shoulders were loaded with hides. Valuable gifts that the sea had bestowed on them. The largest of them came close to Rosalie. A huge, dark shape towering above her. He peered into her face and she smelt his foul breath.

'Yere's a pretty wench,' he called to his friends. 'Will I take she home? My bed'll be cold tonight.'

Instantly, Michael put himself between the man and Rosalie. The man started laughing. He put down his load and a knife flashed in his huge, clumsy fist.

'I've to fight for she, do I?' he jeered.

Michael stood motionless, silent, facing the

man, whose companions crowded round shouting encouragement to their friend. The man lurched suddenly towards Michael with the knife. When Rosalie was certain that the knife had pierced him, Michael sprang lithely to the side. He reached towards the lunging figure, putting his own weight into increasing the man's momentum. The heavy man, caught completely unawares by the sudden movement of his intended victim, fell sprawling on the rocks, his knife striking the slate and deflecting into the black depths of a weed-covered pool.

The crowd began jeering, their loyalties as fickle as the ocean. Rosalie tried to calm her own trembling as Michael turned and stood overshadowing the man. The defeated figure got slowly to his feet, swearing under his breath, his ugly face scowling. Then, as the moon lit the beach again, he showed surprise.

'Michael Pendeen,' he growled. ''Tis Michael Pendeen.'

Michael waved his arm, indicating to the man to get going. Rosalie gasped, then shuddered, for as she saw Michael's hand move, she saw in it a shining blade reflecting the moonlight. Still cursing, the man started hurrying, picking up his hides, glancing at the knife with terror in his eyes. His companions began moving off, muttering amongst themselves.

'He'll nay forget. Be warned. He'll nay forget,' a voice called back.

Michael sheathed his knife quickly, then, taking Rosalie by the hand again, he led her carefully over the lichen-covered rocks, away from the crowds, to an unoccupied part of the beach. His face was angry, his eyes wild.

'As God's my judge I've killed no man,' he breathed, his voice choking with emotion. 'But if any man touches you, I'll kill him where he stands.'

Rosalie pulled the cloak further round her shoulders. The biting wind chilled her body, but her heart had been chilled by the sight of the knives.

'Michael,' she said tentatively, almost afraid of his anger. He lifted his hand, and gently his fingers traced the contour of her cheek, then rested for a moment under her chin.

'"Tis over now, Rosalie,' he said, his voice calm, yet having a strangeness that Rosalie remembered often in the weeks ahead. His meaning was uncertain. 'I shouldn't 've brought you,' he added.

Rosalie lifted the hand that still held hers and pressed it hard. 'I do not think you dragged me here by my hair,' she said quietly.

Michael smiled, then he pulled her closer. She rested her head on his chest and closed her eyes.

When she opened them again, she just stood quite still, leaning on Michael and watching the sea, watching the scattered debris rising and falling with the tide. Her eyes rested for a moment on something white amongst the rocks some distance away. Then she gasped and lifted her head. Michael followed her gaze and saw what she saw. The whiteness was a face. The dark waters lapped uncaringly around the still body of a sailor.

Michael put two firm hands on her shoulders and turned her away from the sight. 'I'll see if he still breathes,' he said. 'Don't look again.'

He crossed the sand quickly and, kneeling by the man, he put a hand over the man's heart, then he turned him over quickly and began pressing hard on his back.

Rosalie tried not to look. She shivered with the cold. She heard voices near her, a woman's, then a man's shouting, and hooves clattering away from the beach.

She glanced down as the incoming tide began swirling at her feet. She was about to step back further when something attracted her attention in the water. She bent to pick it up. Then, as she eyed it closely, a smile came to her lips. It was the horn of a buffalo, part of the ship's sad cargo.

She climbed over the rocks on to a patch of sand a little farther away from the tide. She heard a man shout; then, without warning, a rough hand grabbed her shoulder, another covered her mouth. She tried to call out, to struggle; she felt a knee thrust in her back; she was pushed forward. Her feet slipped, her boots and stockings getting soaked as she stepped unseeing into icy pools. Half-carried, half-dragged, she was taken up to the road.

When the hand was taken from her mouth, she was too stunned to cry out, too enraged to reason properly. Her hands were thrust behind her back, a rope scraped tight around her wrists. Two men lifted her bodily and threw her into a cart. Rosalie landed softly, on the hand-tied figures of other men and women, their faces pale, their eyes wide with terror. Rosalie pushed herself up to her feet. She bent forward as if to climb out of the cart. The rope hurt her wrists and she, Rosalie Harvey, would not be treated in such a way.

A man in the cart put out his foot and pushed her down. 'Sit down, girl,' he grunted. 'They're armed. They'll shoot 'ee.'

Rosalie sat down. She stared at the man. She stared at the white faces around her. The cart gave a sudden jolt, then shot forward, then turned.

'Where are they taking us? Who are they, anyway?' she demanded. She saw two figures now as they edged into the moonlight; two men in uniform driving the cart.

Slowly the truth dawned, the ridiculous, unbelievable truth. She was being arrested, arrested for stealing from the wrecked ship. The horn she had idly picked up on the beach. They must have been watching. For a moment she wanted to laugh, to shout out: 'Do you realise whom you have arrested?' But she knew it was no use. Who would believe her, anyway? She must wait, wait until she saw someone in authority. They would release her as soon as they knew who she was. Michael would come. He would tell them. He would find her soon.

She leaned on the side of the cart, trying to ease herself away from the man who crushed in next to her. It was not cold. The warmth from the bodies around her spread and the sides of the cart were at least protection against the wind. The journey was long. Much further than the ride from Trevia. One woman sobbed pitifully, another muttered continually under her breath.

'Where are they taking us?' Rosalie asked again, her voice sounding strange, muffled by the rumbling of the cart wheels and the shouts of the driver as he whipped the horses up the hill.

'Bodmin Prison, girl.' Her question was answered at last. 'Till morn, then six months more, if you're lucky ... If nay—then a long journey wi' a ship. Transportation, they call it.'

The man who had spoken shook his head slowly. He went on talking, almost to himself, but Rosalie did not hear. Her face had gone deathly white, her whole being was taut with alarm and fear. She had thought a fine. If the worst came to the worst, she could easily pay a fine. But prison, transportation. These were a new world to her. 'Please, God,' she prayed, 'tell Michael where I am.'

The stench of the prison was so vile that Rosalie vomited as soon as they threw her in the cell. The walk along the stone corridor had been a nightmare. The clanging of keys, the cursing, the swearing, the revolting smell of stale alcohol and urine. The vulgar remarks that followed her as she tried to walk with dignity. To Rosalie it was all unreal. She walked in a daze, hardly feeling the floor beneath her feet. Her very existence in question.

Shrieking voices, echoing continually around the walls. Children crying, women sobbing, all mixed with raucous laughter. When the last door was flung open, she was given a push. She fell heavily on to the filthy, reeking straw.

She lay where she fell, not moving, her eyes tight shut. She did not dare to look at the women around her, whose sobbing and shouting stung her ears. The sores from the too-tight rope throbbed though her hands were free. She had tried desperately to tell the warders that she should not be in there, that it was all a mistake. She had told them her name, asked them to check at Trevia. They had laughed in her face, spat on her frock.

'If you'm a guest of Sir Hugh Trevia, then I'm the Prime Minister,' the chief warder had said, roaring loudly at his own humour.

Rosalie wept now in the cell. She tried to tell herself repeatedly: 'Michael will come. He'll find me.' Each time she heard footsteps she looked up hopefully, expecting to see him, but no one came. Then a thought struck her which tore her heart in two with despair. Had Michael been arrested, too? Was that why he did not come? A large rat ran close to her foot. She stifled a scream. Then she closed her eyes again and wished she was dead. Her whole body ached, exhausted, totally spent. She could hold on to consciousness no longer. Her head fell forward on to her knees. She slept where she was, half-sitting, half-lying, her sleep fitful, her dreams horrific.

CHAPTER NINE

Michael stopped pressing the sailor's back and listened for his breath; none came. He turned him over gently, feeling over his heart. The fluttering that had been there when Michael had knelt beside him had gone. The sailor was dead. He closed the staring eyes sadly. The man was little older than himself. Someone, somewhere, would be waiting for him in vain.

Michael stood up slowly, looking out to sea. The sea that he loved and hated all at once. The sea that gave him his living, yet so often took the lives of those who sailed on her. He sighed, then turned towards Rosalie ... Rosalie? He could not see her. She must have moved back from the tide. He crossed the sand quickly to where he had left her. He strained his eyes in the blackness, glancing up at the sky to see if the moon would soon show.

'Rosalie!' He called her name softly. There was no answer. 'Rosalie!' he shouted louder, a sense of alarm forming in his mind.

He crossed the rocks, and walked back as far as the cliff face. Then he listened, perspiration forming on his furrowed brow. The shouting had stopped. The only noise was that of the sea. The moon gave a little light, suddenly, briefly. Enough for Michael to see, to his horror, that the beach was empty, the spoils of the wreck left scattered, full sacks left unattended. He stood still, a terrible fear gripping his heart. Had someone taken her? But why had she not called out? He would have heard her; or would he? Why had the beach emptied so quickly? The coastguards, of course! Even the dragoons. The people had fled for fear of arrest. Had he really been so engrossed in trying to revive the sailor that he had not heard them come?

But where was Rosalie? She would have come to him had she been afraid, not run away. She must have been taken against her will. He sprang into action, jumping from rock to rock, then running until he reached the place where he had left his horse. The horse had gone. He stared disbelievingly at the vacant post. Could Rosalie possibly have taken his horse? He thrust the idea away in disgust. But on foot—how could he possibly find her on foot?

He started running again, climbing the path to Trebarwith village. It was starting to rain, a light, clinging rain blown horizontally by the wind. He reach a nearby farmhouse, and banged angrily on the door, shouting up at the windows. The stables were locked, or he would have taken a horse and gone.

A voice shouted back through the closed door. 'Who be it that wakes we at this hour o' night?'

' 'Tis Michael Pendeen. I need a horse. 'Tis urgent, Adam. My own's been took.'

The door opened slowly, a lamp shone in his eyes. Then a small thin man stepped out quickly, walking towards the stable without speaking.

Michael followed. 'Were you on the beach tonight, Adam?' he asked.

The man looked at him warily. 'Is there any man, ten miles o' here, was nay?'

'Then tell me: the customs men, did they take many away?'

The man nodded, unlocking the door of the stable, hanging the lamp carefully up on a nail. 'Three carts full, I'd say.'

'Did you see them go? Did you see a young girl took? She'd a brown wool cloak and soft golden hair, if her hood was down.'

The man stood for a moment recalling the scene, then his face brightened and he nodded his head slowly. 'There be a wench like that. I marked her hair. 'Tis not often you see such fair hair in these parts. I marked her manner, too; not whining an' crying like the other women. She looked indignant, angry. I mind she stood up in the cart. Then some fellow pushed she down. They'll 've taken she to Bodmin, Michael. You'm not going there after some worthless wench, be you?'

Michael did not answer. He led out a horse, mounting quickly.

'You'll return 'ee tomorrow, Michael,' the man called.

'You've my word on it, Adam,' Michael shouted, already nearing the road.

It was fifteen miles to Bodmin, and a mile or two extra to get money from his home. Michael had no illusions about how Rosalie would be treated, or how she was feeling. He had spent six months in that prison himself when he was barely fifteen. Even now his stomach felt sick at the memory. He felt the sickness for the whole of the ride. Hating himself for what he had done. Thinking nothing of the long, wearying journey. Thinking only of Rosalie, frightened and alone, because he had been careless of her safety for a short, ill-fated time.

The warder who answered the door, after Michael had banged on it for a full quarter of an hour, was much the worse for drink. He needed to lean on the door jamb for support. He hardly listened to Michael's request to see the warder in charge of the women. Michael gave him a guinea. He still did not understand. Four more guineas and the request seemed to become more clear.

Michael was admitted to the prison and taken to a small airless room with a table and two chairs. A middle-aged woman sat at the table. Her head on her arms, she snored loudly. She was not at all pleased to be woken. She stared at a hazy picture of the tall young man in front of her and took a swig out of an almost-empty rum bottle before she spoke.

'Want to buy yer girlfriend out, do 'ee?' she slurred mockingly.

Michael sighed with relief. At least she had heard what he said.

'Not allowed, 'tain't,' the woman went on. 'Lose me job, I would.'

'I'll pay well,' Michael insisted.

'Worth a lot to 'ee, be she?' The woman leaned back on her chair, scrutinising Michael from head to toe.

'Don't look worth much, 'ee don't. Could 'ave 'ee took, fer tryin' to bribe a warder.'

''Twould be throwing money away, if you did; fifty guineas'd feel good in your pocket when you leave at dawn.' Michael tossed the guineas on the table.

The woman picked up a handful and ran them through her fingers. Then she threw back her head and roared with laughter.

'Would na' take twice that,' she screeched,

leaning towards him. 'What's 'er name, this wench?'

'Rosalie Harvey!' Michael answered slowly. He was not sure that Rosalie had given her own name, but he suspected she had tried to get released by using her connection with Trevia. He knew that would not work. Having an arrested member of the gentry in the prison would give the warders great pleasure. He doubted they would have believed her, anyway.

The woman took another drink, then slammed the bottle down on the table. 'Got n' more time t' waste wi' 'ee,' she shouted. 'Three 'undred guineas in me 'and, an' I'll heed it.'

Michael saw the game. He turned to the door. 'No girl's worth that,' he called back, not looking at the woman. When he reached the door, he slammed it behind him, starting back down the long passage.

'Bide yer time,' a voice called behind him, a voice he had counted on hearing.

He turned round to face the woman again. She had her hand on her head. He hoped it was aching like mad.

'Two 'undred an' fifty,' she said. 'An' that's me last offer.'

Michael laughed out loud. He would have paid every penny he had, but if he paid too much, they would suspect Rosalie was someone special, and his chances would wane. He walked back towards the warder, slowly,

119

deliberately. 'I'll give you two hundred now, if you let me get the girl. If you want more, forget the lot. I'll wait till she gets out.'

The woman seized her chance. 'All right, all right. Show me you've got it, then we'll fetch 'er.'

He followed her back into the room and laid the guineas on the table. His face was a blank, his attitude careless. He could not show the intense relief he felt. Nor must he reveal the three hundred more guineas he had still in his money-bag.

When consciousness eased itself upon Rosalie, waves of light and sound came and went, faintly, then louder, clinking of keys, the clang of the iron doors. Voices jeering, footsteps echoing on the stone floor. Then the sensation of movement, of being carried.

She opened her eyes slowly at first. The lights were dim, almost non-existent. Shapes indistinct, veiled. Then, slowly, a face formed above her—a tired, anxious face—and tears of relief rolled freely down her cheeks as she saw she was being carried by Michael Pendeen.

He did not speak when he saw that she had woken, but the lines on his face became a little less intense. She had been so pale, so deep in sleep, when he had lifted her out of the straw, that he had not been sure whether she was sleeping or ill.

'Get 'ee away from yere quick,' the warder called as the last gate clanged shut.

Michael leaned wearily against the stone wall for a moment. He had ridden as never before and there were miles ahead to cover yet.

'Put me down, Michael. I can walk.' He barely heard the whisper that came from Rosalie's dry lips. The street was in complete blackness. He could not see her face. He would be glad enough to give his arms a rest, so he let her feet fall to the ground gently, keeping a firm arm around her waist.

'Are you hurt? Can you ride?' he asked, his voice hardly recognisible, it was so strained.

'I can ride,' she answered, avoiding the first question. For although her body felt bruised from head to foot, it was her pride, her dignity, that was most injured.

'If you can walk a little, my horse's not far. We must get away.'

Rosalie stared in the blackness at the man she could not see. She wanted to throw herself at him, to sob with his arms around her, tell him how horrible it had been; but Michael seemed aloof, almost cold. She let him lead her to where his horse stood waiting, its nostrils still blowing and its coat steaming from the hard ride.

As Michael put his hands on her waist in readiness to lift her up, she spoke slowly. 'Michael, are you angry with me?'

She felt his fingers digging involuntarily into her waist. She heard the deep inhaled gasp of his breath.

'I, angry with you? Why should I be?' he whispered hoarsely.

'Because I've caused you so much trouble. You must be exhausted. You've ridden fifteen miles that I know of. What else you've done, I don't know. You seem so distant.'

'You don't despise me for allowing this to happen?' he asked, surprise showing in his voice.

'Oh, Michael! Of course not!' she cried.

'Rosalie,' he spoke her name as a sigh, 'will I ever forgive myself?'

Rosalie's tiredness did not allow her the cool, clear-headed thoughts of Mistress Rosalie Harvey. She knew relief from mental torture and a feeling of safety that only Michael had ever given her. She knew that she wanted him more than anything else in the world. She slid her arms up his coat and round his neck. She felt his arms tighten around her, then he kissed the tears from her cheeks and he kissed her hair.

'Oh, Michael,' she whispered. 'I love you.'

He held her so tight that she could scarcely breathe as he told her he loved her, and kissed her lips hard and long.

A sudden sound pierced the silence around them, a whistled tune, then heavy footsteps. Michael released his grip quickly, whispering in her ear, 'On the horse, we must be gone.'

The hooves clattered loudly on the cobblestones as they rode out of Bodmin.

Michael rode fast, and Rosalie clung to him tightly just to stay on the horse. When they had left the town, he slowed the pace.

Rosalie's thoughts were confused by the sudden dash.

'Michael,' she said, 'how did you get me out of prison?'

'I bribed the warders,' he said flatly.

'With money?'

'Aye.'

'I'll repay you,' she said. 'How much did you need?'

He did not answer. Rosalie sighed. She was too weary to argue now. She would make him tell her later. She leaned her head against him and closed her eyes. It had been a strange and terrible night, but now she was safe. All she wanted was to stay close, very close, to Michael.

CHAPTER TEN

Michael shielded his eyes against the bright mid-day sun. It threw warm shafts of light across the room, striking the bare white walls with squares of glowing yellow. Only Michael's still shadow broke the pattern as he stood watching the scurrying clouds overhead. The tell-tale sign of a bitter easterly wind. He knew that the warmth from the sun was deceptive. The granite farmhouse nestled snugly in a wooded valley, sheltered on all sides.

The large kettle began singing on the fire. Michael lifted it carefully to make fresh tea. He had heard movements in the bedroom above and he guessed that Rosalie would soon be coming down.

He had brought her to his family's home for several reasons; reasons which, in his weariness on the long ride from Bodmin, he had been unable to define. Rosalie had raised no objection when, as the dim light of dawn eased their way, he had ridden down into the Pendeen valley. When his widowed mother had been woken, had helped Rosalie to undress, she had been grateful. A secretive return to Trevia, the cold unknowing eyes of the servants; these would have been cruel compared with the understanding welcome she was given by Michael's family.

As Michael heard footsteps on the stairs, his heart missed a beat. He watched the door with a desperate hope. The hope that into the room would step Mistress Rosalie Harvey, demanding to be taken to Trevia at once. The door opened slowly. As his gaze met her eyes he knew instantly that his hope was shattered. For here was the same young girl he had held in his arms in the lightless street outside Bodmin prison. He knew that his own pain would be greater, his words twice as hard to say, twice as hard to hear. He saw that she was wearing his sister's frock. His mother had taken her own and washed it immediately to rid it of the prison odour.

Michael smiled at her. He pulled out a chair at the bare wooden table. His eyes still showed tiredness, he had slept little, but Rosalie saw only the light in them as he watched her every movement. To her, Michael stood as a Greek god, young and tall, with his shoulder-length black hair shining. He wore the silk shirt she had made for him and his best leather breeches. At his slim waist was a strong leather belt fastened by the silver buckle he had won in the wrestling match. She had forgotten the knife that had been pulled from that belt on Trebarwith beach. Rosalie sat down, glancing enquiringly around, expecting another voice.

'My brother Tom's taken Mother to Bodmin—to the market. We're alone, Rosalie. Would you like tea?'

'Yes, please.'

'And what does Mistress Harvey like for breakfast?' he asked gently. 'We've bacon, bread. If you wish for eggs, I'll see if there's any yet.'

Rosalie sipped her tea, then she looked at the blazing log fire, at the black cooking pots on the hob.

'I would like bacon, but—' She faltered.

Michael stood up, turned to the fire and,

putting two rashers of bacon in a frying-pan, he fixed it over the flames.

'Michael,' she said, 'you should not be cooking breakfast for me.'

He turned his head towards her and smiled. 'Have you ever cooked bacon?' he asked.

She shook her head.

'Then today we'll do as we're able. I'll need your help in a while.'

When Rosalie had eaten, Michael cleared the table without speaking. Then he took an envelope from the mantelshelf and opened it.

'I've written to the captain of the *Padstow Mermaid*. I'd like you to read it—to tell me if 'tis badly written or if the spelling is wrong.' He gave her the letter. 'If you think 'tis so, I'll write it again.'

She read the letter slowly. It was a request that the captain be generous in his dealings with his two young crew members, with a promise that he would be well rewarded if they were returned safely to England at his earliest convenience. The writing was bold. She saw he had taken great pains with the letters. She knew he had had no schooling. All his achievements were the results of his own meticulous efforts.

'There are a few slight mistakes in the spelling, Michael,' she said, 'but I do not think it necessary for you to write it again.'

He smiled. 'I've taken a liberty in offering a reward without asking you first, but as you've the money I think 'twould help your brothers if such a promise is made.'

Rosalie nodded. 'I'd have done the same myself, had I known where to write.'

'A friend of mine sails from Port Isaac for America tomorrow. I mind 'tis likely his ship'll put in harbour at Boston before the *Padstow Mermaid* sails. I'll ask him to convey the letter for me, if 'tis possible.'

'Thank you.'

Michael put the letter back on the shelf. Then he sat down again. He looked straight into Rosalie's blue eyes; and had she seen it, his hand was gripping the seat of his chair like a vice.

'I wish to speak of you now, Rosalie,' he said, keeping his voice even and calm with difficulty. 'There's little more you can do for your brothers in Cornwall. We've assured ourselves that they're on their way to America. Till they return, there's naught you can do.' His eyes almost faltered, he wanted to look away from her, so he did not see the pain that he would put on her face. But he kept his gaze steady and went on.

' 'Twould be better if you returned to your home. Better for you—and for—me.' The last word was barely audible. He saw the light leave her eyes. Her face grew pale.

' 'Twould be easy for me to say I wish you to stay in Cornwall—that we could go on meeting as we've done. Last night—when I kissed

127

you—I was following my heart, not my head—and you were doing the same.'

A log fell noisily in the grate. He got up and put another one on almost mechanically. When he sat down again, Rosalie was staring at the table, twisting her handkerchief between her fingers.

'You are telling me I must return to Nottingham—and marry Robert,' she said slowly.

'Aye.'

'And you do not wish to see me again.'

Michael swallowed hard. If there had been no wooden table between them, he would have taken her in his arms. He thanked God for the table.

'You're so young, Rosalie. You've found excitement, adventure in the time we've spent together. Last night was the payment for my foolish recklessness. What future'd there be if you stay. When my boat is built, I'll work hard. I'll be away at sea for most of the time. Our worlds are as far apart as—the earth is from the moon. You'd soon tire of your Cornish smuggler. When you return home—you'll soon forget I exist. A memory now and then perchance, but no more. If you doubt what I say, stay here for two days, a week? See how I live. How little our lives even touch. My mother'll welcome you.'

Rosalie got slowly to her feet. She went to the window and, shielding her eyes as Michael had done, she watched the sheep grazing in the lee of the hillside, huddled together against the wind.

Michael's hand let go of his chair. He pushed it roughly away. The table was no longer between them, only space; and space could be crossed easily. Rosalie turned as she felt his arm round her, and she sobbed with her head on his chest.

When the fitful shaking had stopped, he washed her face as if she were a child.

Then he sighed. 'Will I take you to Trevia or will you stay here? I sent a message this morn to say that Mistress Harvey left Trevia very early and would let them know her intentions later.' He smiled. 'I feared if you were missed from your bed, I might be charged with kidnapping. A hanging crime.'

'May I stay, at least until tomorrow? Trevia seems so cold, so unwelcoming now. And, Michael—I owe you money.'

'You owe me nothing.'

Rosalie frowned. 'Buying me out of prison must have cost much. The money you have is for your boat. I'll not have you use it for me.'

Michael took her hands between his own. 'Would you have me suffer even more than I do already? 'Twill take me three months, no more, to earn the money again. Let me at least take that as a punishment that I let such a thing happen to you. I must lose the one who's dearest in my heart; would you have me also lose my pride?'

Rosalie smiled. 'I think you read too much of William Shakespeare. Your honour overrides your common sense. But if that's really what you wish, I'll abide by it.'

Michael started suddenly. 'Your books, Rosalie, you must take them with you when you go.'

She shook her head. 'Keep them, Michael, as a gift. You allow me to give you so little.'

He raised his hands with exaggerated surprise. 'A shirt, and books!' he said. 'I'm rich indeed.'

They heard the cart rattling down the hill. Michael put the kettle back on the fire and his mother came in, glad to be out of the cold. She gave Rosalie a warm smile, then looked anxiously at Michael.

'James's sick, Michael. Meg sent word. She canna' manage the farm wi' they bairns an' a sick man. Will 'ee go?'

Michael sighed, nodding slowly. He looked at Rosalie, the time he had left with her getting less and less.

'James's my elder brother,' he said. 'He and Meg have a farm on the other side of the moor.' He turned to his mother. 'Rosalie'll stay till tomorrow, Mother.' He glanced at Rosalie. 'She's not used to farm work. I think the Pendeens can manage as always.'

His mother nodded. 'I understand, Michael,' she said. 'We'll be pleased to have she stay.'

Mary Pendeen watched her son as he prepared for his journey across the moor. When he had arrived home at dawn, so exhausted, with a strange, sleeping maid in his arms, she had asked no questions. She had seen the look between them when the maid woke. Whilst helping the maid to undress, she had seen the silk petticoats that she wore. She understood now why her son had so much sadness in his eyes; why Rosalie had been crying.

Michael was ready to go, far too soon for Rosalie. The packs ready on his horse and his coat on against the wind.

'Get your cloak, Rosalie,' he said. 'Walk a short way with me.'

They walked only far enough to be out of sight of the house before Michael stopped. He loosed his horse to graze at the side of the path, then took Rosalie in his arms.

'No tears, my love,' he said quietly. 'Let me remember you smiling.' He kissed her gently, knowing full well it would be the last time. 'Tom'll take you back to Trevia,' he said. 'Just tell him when you're ready to go.' He laughed a little ruefully. 'He's to go out tonight to do some moonlighting for me.'

'You were going smuggling tonight?' Rosalie asked.

He nodded. 'I was riding a cargo into Wadebridge from the coast, but Tom'll do it.'

'What will you do on your brother's farm?'

131

'Milk the cows mostly, keep an eye on the sheep on the moor. Anything to make my sister-in-law's burden easier till James's well again.'

'Is your sister-in-law pretty?'

Michael raised his dark eyebrows and laughed. 'I've never considered it. I suppose she is. She's older than I. We're good friends, though.' He kissed her forehead impulsively. 'I'll tell her about you. She'll understand.'

The horse threw back his head and let out a loud neigh.

Michael looked up at the sky. 'We'll have rain soon,' he said. 'I must be gone.' His eyes searched her face as if wanting to commit each portion to his memory. 'You will be gone before I return.' The words were a plea more than a question.

Rosalie nodded. 'From here, and from Trevia. Take care how you ride, Michael.'

His black eyes were grave for a moment. 'There's many things I've left unsaid, but I think you know them. I'll see that I, or at least one of my brothers, is at Padstow when your brothers return. We'll put them on the stage to you. Be happy, my love, then I'll be content.'

He smiled suddenly, his black eyes flashed. He took a sweeping bow and kissed her hand, knowing it would make her laugh. Then quickly he caught his horse and mounted. Without looking back, he rode out into the wind, her laughing face already a picture in his memory.

CHAPTER ELEVEN

Rosalie put her hands over her ears and stared. The noise around her made her head ache. The monotonous banging of the great hammers. The grating and clanging of the cog wheels. The creaking of the giant water wheel as it was pushed slowly round by the churning waters of the River Leen. She followed the direction of the machinery slowly. Then she entered the white plastered workroom of the Harveys' spinning mill, using the keys she had found in her father's desk.

She had never been to this part before, although she was ashamed to admit it now. Visits to the mill had always begun and ended at the manager's office. Today she had entered by the back door, unannounced, unexpected. She stood in the corner, watching. No one noticed her. Too busy were her workers. Too busy were the children, running errands, crawling beneath the great length of the spinning frame. Cleaning fluff from the machine and the floor, or changing over the long reels.

She watched, horrified, as a young boy carrying a cup of water in his hand became caught underneath a machine. She listened to his cries of terror as the machine was stopped; the child pulled roughly to safety. Then the moment was broken, the anonymity lost, as Mr Jennings came into the room and saw to his astonishment his elegant employer standing silently observing.

'Mistress Harvey!' he cried, his hands still gesticulating his amazement. 'I—I did not know you had returned from Cornwall.'

'I only arrived yesterday, Mr Jennings,' she said, deciding instantly not to apologise for her unexpected visit. Mr Jennings fingered his small moustache nervously, acutely disturbed by her method of entry. He kept glancing at the usually locked door which Rosalie had left ajar.

'Why are the doors kept locked, Mr Jennings?' she asked, looking him straight in the eye.

'Why, Mistress Harvey!' he exclaimed with surprise. 'The doors have always been kept locked.'

Rosalie tilted her chin up a little higher. 'I know, Mr Jennings; but why?'

Richard Jennings looked at the doors, then back at Rosalie. 'To keep the workers in, Mistress Harvey,' he said hurriedly. 'If the doors were not locked they would find any excuse to go out for a rest, especially in the summer when it is hot. In some mills they do not allow the windows to be opened at all, but here we do allow a little fresh air in when it is very hot,' he said defensively.

Rosalie nodded. 'I see.'

Mr Jennings tried ushering her politely towards his office door; Rosalie stood her ground.

'I would like to—' She was about to say inspect, then she changed her mind. 'I would like to—talk to the workers,' she said. 'Alone, if you please.'

Mr Jennings' face reddened. She was not sure whether it was with anger or embarrassment.

'If you have complaints with my work, Mistress Harvey, I would prefer to be told,' he said, keeping his voice low.

Rosalie gave him what she hoped was a reassuring smile.

'My complaints are not against you, Mr Jennings,' she said. 'They are more against myself. I may wish to make a few changes. If you will continue with your work, I will see you in your office when I am finished.'

Mr Jennings gave a slight bow, then left her somewhat uneasily. She spent the whole morning talking to the work-people. She was shocked at the long hours without breaks, by the conditions of their homes. When she had had the children together in groups she had learned a great deal about the people who worked in her mill.

Yet, whilst they were talking to her, there was always another voice in her head. Michael's voice, telling her what it was like for a ten-year-old child to be exhausted by work.

Michael's voice at Padstow saying, 'Thirteen hours a day, locked in from morn till night!' Then his voice forcing itself unwanted, a strained, tired voice; telling her she must return to Nottingham, never see him again. She swallowed hard; brought her mind back to the present, to the young apprentices, making the most of their freedom of speech.

When the stagecoach had rumbled over the River Trent and Rosalie had seen the imposing sight of Nottingham Castle, she had sighed with relief. It had been barely visible in the cold sunless light of December, but it had meant she was almost home. Charlesworth Hall had been warm, welcoming, as she had known it would be. Alice Morley, who had been with the Harveys before Rosalie was born, had wept openly to have her safe home again. She and Rosalie had always been close; the old woman was the nearest to a mother that Rosalie could remember.

Throughout the three-day-long journey, Rosalie had been planning how she could improve working conditions in the mill, her tormented mind seeking desperately to keep occupied, to overcome the haunting emptiness in her heart. As she looked at the girls and boys before her now, she did not see workers who owed her their work for the food and accommodation she provided for them. She saw children with as much right to education and happiness as she and her brothers had had.

She intended to see that they got it.

Mr Jennings was hardly surprised when Rosalie announced to him that the doors were no longer to be locked.

'I wish all the workers to take a half-hour break at midday,' she went on. Mr Jennings moved uncomfortably around in his chair, hoping that that was the worst news, but fearing it was not.

'All children, whether apprenticed or not, are to be given one hour per day of tuition in reading, writing and arithmetic.' Mr Jennings felt decidedly faint. He took a little snuff. Rosalie explained that she personally would find a teacher and supply the books. 'I also intend to provide toys and games to the children's accommodation.'

Mr Jennings was speechless. All the excuses he had been thinking of, whilst Rosalie was talking, expired into thin air. He found himself agreeing to the proposals without the least idea how he could manage to give so much time off to the workers of an already failing mill. Rosalie was pleased with her morning's work. She even allowed herself the thought that Michael would have been pleased, had he known. When her carriage had returned her safely home, she wrote out an advertisement for a teacher.

Sending her groom with the advertisement to the *Nottingham Journal*, she also gave him a letter to take to Rayleigh House, telling Robert she had returned. She then had luncheon and changed carefully into her prettiest afternoon gown to wait for him.

Michael had been right. Their love had no future; just a beautiful dream filled with daring and adventure. As mistress of Rayleigh, she would have security and the love of a man whom she at least liked and respected. She thought of Lucy Trevia, married to a man whom she had grown to despise for his lack of kindness and unfaithfulness. Marriage to Robert would be easy compared to the life that Lucy had. But, even as she heard hoofbeats on the drive, she knew that her relationship with Robert would never be the same. There would always be a secret between them. There would always be Cornwall and the love she had had for her Cornish smuggler.

* * *

Robert straightened his white muslin cravat carefully as he dressed to go riding. He picked up his riding-crop and took a last look in the mirror. Yes, his new maroon velvet riding jacket was definitely a good choice. He sighed deeply. How he wished Rosalie was here to go riding with him. Her letters were so curt, so uninformative. He was tired of defending her to his mother.

The nearness of Christmas brought little promise of seasonal cheer to Robert. He had not enjoyed the weeks since his return from Cornwall. He had had time to think, time to reminisce about the past; to plan for the future. He had decided that when—and that was the question—when Rosalie returned, he would take her to London.

If anyone was to blame for Rosalie's liking for independence, her boyish behaviour, then surely he must accept the larger part of the blame. Had he not always treated her as an equal as they jumped fences together and rode neck and neck for the boundary at the edge of Sherwood Forest? He smiled when he remembered one occasion barely a year ago when he had decided to walk to Charlesworth Hall.

Part-way through the wood, he had been astonished to see Rosalie sitting on a branch half-way up a tree. She had not seen him and he had hidden, to discover that she and her brothers were playing hide-and-seek. When Ben had found her, she had jumped down quite fearlessly, proving unquestionably that she was not unused to the action. He had shown himself then, and she had become the perfect lady in a second, hurriedly hiding the tear in her gown.

It had been on her eighteenth birthday that she had started hiding her indiscretions from him. Until then, she would run quite openly to meet him, recounting excitedly every detail of the antics of herself and her brothers. Being so much in her company, he had hardly noticed how she was changing. When he had seen her in Cornwall he had noticed a new radiance, a new fire. Never before had he seen her looking so beautiful. He had decided she deserved more than the presumptuous proposal he had made in such haste. Yes, he would take her to London; take her dancing, to the theatre. And when she was enchanted by the music, by the gaiety, he would choose a suitable time to propose again.

He heard hoofbeats on the drive and glanced out of the window. The Harveys' groom! What could—? Robert did not wait to guess. He descended the stairs three at a time and was outside on the steps before the groom reached the door. He read the letter quickly, thanked the man, then ran to get his own horse from the stables.

Rosalie was in the library when Robert was announced. She was sorting out books that might be suitable for the school. She had decided at the last minute that she would find it easier to be well occupied when Robert arrived. She could then switch the conversation as she pleased.

When he stepped into the library, she looked straight into his eyes. Yes, there was a light in them. A look of joy, of admiration, as he took in the cornflower-blue gown she had chosen because it matched her eyes. But his eyes were not compelling, they betrayed Robert's heart, but her own did not answer.

'You look well, Rosalie. I hope the journey did not tire you too much.' He glanced at the piles of books and smiled. 'Are you dusting the shelves or preparing for an auction sale?'

'I'm sorting out books for the school at the mill,' she said.

Robert raised his eyebrows, but did not comment.

'Perhaps you would like to help me, or are you riding somewhere special?' she said, noticing his new jacket.

Robert was relieved; at least she had asked him to stay, which was more than she did in Cornwall. He offered to help. He was not aware that there was a school at the mill, but then, if she had asked him to help her sort embroidery silks he would have done it.

Rosalie explained her intentions for the mill. She said nothing about her brothers, so Robert did not ask. If there were more news he was sure she could have told him. She did not mention Cornwall, either. He was pleased. If she was making plans for the mill, then she was not planning to return there. He started sorting books.

Rosalie was surprised at Robert's sudden interest in the mill. She had expected disapproval for her plans, yet here he was actually helping. He even said he knew of a teacher who might be willing to take the post. With his help she could do even more.

Christmas at home without the boys would mean nothing. If she could buy small presents for the children at the mill—to actually give them out herself—then she would have the joy of giving as well as knowing they would have at least one present. She wondered why she had not thought of it before.

She watched Robert scanning the shelves; she smiled to herself. Then suddenly she heard Michael's voice telling her how far their worlds were apart. 'If I do this for the children, am I not bringing our worlds nearer, Michael?' she whispered. Robert turned, thinking she had spoken to him, but he saw she was staring unseeing out of the window, a smile on her lips. He could not know that Rosalie was feeling the wind on her face, smelling the salt in the air. Hearing Michael laughing as he lifted her down from the rocks. Michael; always ahead of her needs, always knowing what she could manage alone, always knowing when she needed his help. Rosalie sighed—then the colour rushed to her cheeks as she saw Robert watching her. She smiled defensively and told him how well his new jacket suited him. Robert's vanity was appeased. He forgot the strange look in her eyes and got on with the search.

Rosalie was kept busy during the next month. Christmas came and was gone so fast that, although she dare not admit it, she scarcely missed her brothers. The teacher was well installed in the mill. The workers' mid-day break was well established. But the sales of yarn were not improving. Mr Jennings was a worried man. The introduction of the mules into the mill was more difficult than he had anticipated. Without more capital, he feared the mill would close. And Mistress Harvey was spending her capital on schools, teachers, books and better clothes for the apprentices.

When Robert asked Rosalie to go to London with him, she accepted immediately, much to his astonishment. London was cold, freezing cold; basking in late February snow, snow that was churned into brown ridges by the wheels of the carriages and carts. Tradesmen delivered their wares on sledges until the weak sunlight became gradually stronger, the days a little warmer.

For Rosalie, February in London was not cold. Whenever she ventured out she was well wrapped in warm cloaks, muffs and boots. London was warm, friendly and exciting. She was whirled off her feet at the extravagant balls, amazed by the numbers of young men who came calling to invite her to join their theatre party, or to take tea with their sisters.

As February became March, the weather improved. Activities included drives in the blue phaeton of Charles Nelson, son of her host and hostess, Mr and Mrs John Nelson. Robert was staying at his club. He was a little disillusioned by Rosalie's immediate popularity. Rosalie rather liked Charles Nelson. He danced well and drove his horses fast and with great expertise. But then, she rather liked Philip Warneford, too. By the end of April, Rosalie's week was well organised between balls with Charles, dinner with Robert, theatre with Philip and party, riding in the Row; and so it went on. Robert became restless, tired of the social round, wishing for his own horses and open country. Seeing more and more of Rosalie's time taken away from him, knowing full well that he was long overdue a visit to attend to the affairs of his estate, he tried to persuade Rosalie to come home with him, but she pleaded to stay in London. He went home alone.

Philip Warneford became a daily visitor at the Nelsons' home. He had always been a close friend of Charles, but Rosalie saw a growing friction between them and realised to her dismay that she was the cause of it.

On April the 8th a large bouquet of flowers arrived for Rosalie. She came downstairs to find Charles Nelson pacing the floor in the drawing-room. He stopped walking when he saw her; indicating towards the table.

'Those came for you this morning,' he said, trying to sound casual. It would have been more usual for him to have them sent up for her, not to have left them until she came down.

Rosalie turned her back to him whilst she read the card. She suspected he was wanting to see her face as she read. She felt annoyed. She wondered if he had dared to read it himself.

The flowers were from Philip. An invitation to the theatre at Drury Lane that evening, then to dine with him after. She put the card carefully back into the envelope, picked up the flowers and started to leave the room.

'Mistress Harvey, Rosalie.' Charles Nelson's face looked in pain. 'I was hoping that you would dine with me tonight,' he said.

Rosalie gave him her warmest smile. 'I am most fearfully sorry, Charles,' she said. 'But I have already accepted an invitation from Philip. Perhaps another evening.'

Charles did not attempt to hide the disappointment on his face. He bowed and left the room without speaking.

After luncheon, Robert was announced. Rosalie was quite glad to see him back. He smiled and greeted everybody cordially, but there were worried lines on his face.

It was not until after tea that he had a chance to speak to Rosalie alone. He told her the news from home, then he hesitated and his face became tense.

'Robert, what is the matter?' she asked anxiously.

'I dined at my club before I came here, Rosalie. I heard some rather disturbing news there. I feel I should tell you of it.' He broke off, not being sure whether she might know already.

Rosalie stared at him. 'Tell me,' she insisted impatiently.

'There is a duel being fought, at dawn tomorrow.'

'A duel!' Rosalie's eyes shone with delight. 'How exciting!'

'I fear you will not think it so when I tell you who is duelling.'

Rosalie did not speak. The possibilities raced through her mind.

'Charles Nelson has challenged Philip Warneford. He has accepted. If you do not know already, they are fighting over you.'

Rosalie sat stunned, speechless. The flowers! The look on Charles' face when he had left!

Robert put a hand on her arm. 'Shall we walk in the garden? I find it a little close in here.'

Rosalie nodded. She got to her feet and took the arm that Robert offered. What had she done? She had never meant it to be like this. She had enjoyed the attention they had lavished on her. Robert had seemed a little dull against the elegant young men of London. She had meant to tease him a little. Then more and more she had enjoyed their company. She had played them a little against each other. Yes, she admitted that. But a duel. It was quite ridiculous. It must be stopped. They reached a quiet arbour and Rosalie accepted Robert's suggestion that they sat down.

'I think,' he said, 'that you must tell me what

has gone on whilst I have been away. Do you have any intention of marrying either of these two young bucks?'

'Marry?' Rosalie was astonished. 'Why, of course I do not.'

Robert closed his eyes with intense relief. 'Then may I suggest that you return home. Then we may be able to stop this foolishness.' He smiled a little. 'I shall probably find myself challenged by both of them now.'

Rosalie looked shocked again. 'Oh, Robert, you would not fight?' she cried.

'I would fight for your safety, or your honour, but not for your love. That is something you must give freely.'

Rosalie leaned back on the seat, closing her eyes. 'I have been very foolish, Robert. I have treated you badly.'

Robert took her hand. She did not pull it away. 'It is the future that most concerns me, Rosalie. Your future and mine, but perhaps now is not the time.'

Rosalie opened her eyes and looked up into his. Robert could keep his calmness no longer. His arm went round her; he kissed her. She closed her eyes and kissed him back. A light breeze began stirring the trees, a rustling ran through them like an arrow. Rosalie leaned her head on Robert's shoulder and listened.

The breeze became suddenly louder to Rosalie. It became a fierce wind stinging her cheeks, blowing her hair. She heard laughter;

her own laughter, then Michael's. Robert was kissing her again, and suddenly it was wrong. She closed her eyes; tried to pretend he was Michael, but she could not do that for the rest of her life.

Robert was stunned when she pushed him away. Had she been any woman but Rosalie he would have thought she was playing games with him. He rested his arm on the back of the seat, regarding her face with consternation. He saw her eyes were wet, she was crying. He took out a white handkerchief and gave it to her.

'Will you at least tell me what is wrong, Rosalie?' he begged. 'Do you consider me too—too forward, because I kissed you? I have tried to be patient—but I find it harder each time I am with you.'

Rosalie said nothing, she stared miserably at the floor.

'Is it Rayleigh? Are you worried about my mother?'

Rosalie lifted her head and looked up at him through misty eyes. 'Please stop being so kind, Robert. I do not deserve it. I can never marry you because I do not love you.'

'Never!' he exclaimed with dismay. Then he was silent; he looked away from her and stared into the apple trees, unseeing.

Rosalie hated herself for making him so unhappy. He was taking an envelope from his coat pocket. She watched mystified as he turned back towards her. He looked worried, as though he had made a decision he did not much like.

'I had hoped to spare you this, Rosalie,' he said. 'But, if we return to Nottingham tomorrow as I fear we must, you will learn of it anyway. Your mill is in trouble. You may have to declare bankruptcy.'

Rosalie stared at the solicitor's heading on the notepaper, then she looked at Robert with astonishment. 'Why did they write to you?' she asked.

'A request of your father, Rosalie. One I have always known. If there were ever a question of financial trouble for you, I was to be told first.' He gave a deep sigh. 'I had really hoped not to do this. If you were to marry me, knowing your concern for the people of the mill, I intended to invest capital in it for you. But—' His brown eyes turned sadly away from her. 'In view of what you have just told me, I do not know what to do. My financial advisers have warned me against it—but I would have been willing to take the risk—for you.'

Rosalie stared at him, confused, distraught. 'Does this mean I'll have no money at all, Robert?'

'You will have what is left of your own capital, but I fear you have spent rather a lot—'

'That's why you insisted on paying for my gowns for this visit, Robert. You knew about the mill.'

Robert nodded, then he smiled. 'Rosalie,' he

said, 'I will not persist in asking you to marry me, but I want you to know that the offer is always open. If for some reason which I confess I do not understand, you will not marry me, then you have my assurance that I will not see you short of money. I will make you an allowance, whatever you do.'

Rosalie looked away from him. 'Whatever she did.' If only she could tell him what she really longed to do. Oh, why did it have to be Robert she was hurting? Suddenly she was faced with a terrible choice. The jobs of the people at the mill—or her own happiness. Her head was throbbing, her thoughts confused.

'Will you give me time to consider, Robert?' she said. 'I will leave London with you tomorrow. I shall send a message to Philip saying I am unable to accept his invitation tonight as I am leaving. I will do the same to Charles. Do you think this will stop the duel?'

Robert nodded.

'And, Robert, you will keep well away from them both, won't you?'

CHAPTER TWELVE

Lucy Trevia was surprised when Rosalie was announced so early in the morning. She was breakfasting alone in her London house, rejoicing in the fact that her husband had allowed her to stay in London. He usually insisted she return to Cornwall whilst he was away, but yesterday he sailed to Italy—on business, or so he said. She was sadly aware that she could not attend the balls she loved or indeed take much part in social life at all. She could at least go to the theatre and entertain her friends at the house. She was brimming with good humour, sparkling with vivacity.

When Rosalie was shown in to her she saw instantly that something was wrong. Rosalie's face was tired and drawn; her eyes still red from crying, despite her efforts to conceal it. Lucy pulled up a chair and poured coffee for her before she spoke.

'Drink the coffee, then tell me when you are ready,' she said gently.

Rosalie did as she said, then smiled a wan smile.

'I had to come to you, Lucy,' she said. 'There is no one else to whom I could talk.'

'Then tell me, my dear. You know you can trust me. Hugh is away, so we will not be disturbed.'

Rosalie told her what had passed between Robert and herself on the evening before. 'I am completely torn between responsibility to others and what I feel myself,' she said miserably. 'If I do not marry Robert, then not only may the mill people lose their jobs, but also my brothers will not have the mill my father left them.'

Lucy was frowning. There was something she did not understand. 'How are you so sure you do not love Robert?' she asked. 'You do like him, which is more than I did Hugh when I married him.'

Rosalie stared into her coffee cup for a moment, then she looked up at Lucy sadly.

'Robert—is—an elder brother to me, Lucy. He is no different to Peter. I've always turned to him for advice or help; he has always been a good friend—but I cannot think of him as a lover. I only wish I could.'

'There is someone else you have met in London?' Lucy enquired warily.

Rosalie shook her head. 'No, in Cornwall,' she confessed.

Lucy smiled. 'I thought as much when we were there. You were so changed suddenly. But who is he? You would not let me introduce you to any of the eligible men in the district. How did you meet him?' she asked eagerly.

Rosalie did not answer for quite a while. She smoothed down her skirts as she always did when she was anxious.

'He is—' She hesitated, choosing her words carefully. 'He has his own boat. He fishes—and takes cargoes. And I love him, Lucy.' She did not mention smuggling.

Lucy did not show shock or even surprise. Rosalie was grateful. Lucy walked to the window. She was silently thoughtful; then she wheeled round quickly and spoke in a quiet, calm voice.

'You know that my marriage to Hugh has brought me no happiness, Rosalie,' she said. 'When I was eighteen, I thought I was in love with my sister's tutor. My parents dismissed him and arranged my marriage to Hugh. They told me the most important thing in marriage was security. Now, I have all the security I shall ever need. I have a well-respected husband whom I dislike; and who blames me entirely because we have no children. I have never had his love, nor he mine. If I were to live those years again, I would at least have liked the opportunity to find out whether or not I did love Andrew Yeomans.' She waved her arms defensively. 'Oh, I know I like expensive clothes, London life; but these are compensations for my marriage, for the bitterness I feel.'

'But, Lucy! You had only yourself to consider. I had thought I might forget Michael. That he was right when he said I would do so, but I have not. Yet what of the mill? Of my brothers?'

Lucy went over and pulled the bell cord. When the servant arrived, she asked for the carriage to be brought.

'We will visit a friend of mine,' she said, smiling. 'He is a genius with figures and well informed on such things as mills. We will ask his advice.'

Lucy's friend was more than just helpful. He went with them to the London office of Rosalie's solicitors. After studying the accounts of the mill for two solid hours, he told her quite definitely that even were Robert to put capital into the mill, it would still fail. An owner was required who had skill at business, plenty of money and a great deal of experience of the trade. If the mill were sold, he considered it most likely that someone with other interests in the trade would purchase it. In his opinion, this would be the best way to guarantee jobs for the employees.

'Could I make any conditions if the mill were sold?' Rosalie asked, a little lightness creeping into her voice.

'What sort of conditions?' the man asked.

'That the school be continued. I could perhaps still pay for the teacher myself.'

The man was thoughtful. 'I should think that would be possible,' he said. 'Your solicitors would advise you better on that point, Mistress Harvey.'

When Lucy and Rosalie returned to Lucy's house, Lucy waved an accusing finger at her guest.

'I have seen that look in your eye before, Rosalie,' she said. 'The time you were working out how to persuade Robert to leave Cornwall. Now I know why, of course. You are scheming again. Is it me you are planning to get rid of this time?' she teased.

Rosalie smiled, a glimmer of hope showing. She had suddenly remembered long-forgotten words of her father.

He had told her that he had put more money in trust for her brothers than her.

'You will marry, Rosalie,' he had said. 'The boys will need to support their wives and families. By the time they are twenty-one, they will have enough money to start another business if they wish. Just in case the mill goes through.' Just in case. Right up till now she had forgotten those words. Forgotten that her father had ever mentioned the possibility.

Suddenly, she was free. She looked at Lucy with such relief and excitement in her eyes that Lucy burst out laughing.

'You're welcome to stay at Trevia as long as you wish,' she said. 'But I'll not come with you.'

CHAPTER THIRTEEN

Spring in Cornwall. Wild gorse along the hedgerows. Masses of pale yellow primroses filling the lanes and banks. The tall green stalks shooting up amongst them, waiting their turn to burst into bluebells. Rosalie sighed. How beautiful it all was; and today the sea was so very blue. She stood on the beach at Trebarwith, watching the water strike the rocks, its force so great that it changed instantly into a white frothy spray, thrown skywards for a fleeting second before cascading down.

How she loved Cornwall. But where was Michael? She had been at Trevia for three weeks already; not a sight nor sound of him had she had. She was always expecting him to appear from nowhere as he had before. But he had not come. She had been sure that the news that Mistress Harvey was back at Trevia would reach him. She had walked in the garden there every day. She had walked down the street in Camelford, trying hard to keep her gaze from the group of men sitting draining their tankards outside the Bedford Arms, yet desperately hoping that one of them was Michael, that he would see her and follow when she turned down by the river. But no one had come.

She closed her eyes for a moment, smelling the salt sea, remembering the last time she had stood on this beach; the night of the wreck, when she had been taken to Bodmin Prison. The night when Michael had kissed her and told her he loved her.

She opened her eyes slowly and gazed out to the huge hulk of the Gull Rock. The white billowing sails of a schooner came from behind it. Her heart gave a lurch; her pulse quickened as it always did whenever she saw a ship. Perhaps Michael was away on a long voyage.

He could have sailed for Spain, Italy, or—She turned away from the foaming ocean. Then she climbed steadily to where her horse stood waiting. She rode up to Trebarwith village, through Delabole and down into the Pendeens' valley. If Michael did not want her, then at least she must know.

At the gate, she stood for a moment, her hand on the catch. She took in the scene around her: the solid granite farmhouse with its worn paintwork, its small square windowpanes. She had left Michael's home in winter when the naked trees were bowed low by fierce winds, when the bare soil lay dormant, the barn half-full of hay. Today, there was still a wind moving the trees; a lighter, warmer wind. The trees that it swayed were thick in bud, bowed low now by heavy blossoms. The slatey soil at the side of the house had been hoed. Young green shoots pushed their way towards the warm May sunlight. Against the cowshed a long-handled spade leaned idly. The barn stood empty, waiting.

Rosalie glanced up at the blue mackerel sky as she pushed open the gate. A plump thrush settled on a nearby apple tree rendering a tuneful welcome. Everything promised new birth, new awakening in this Cornish spring; yet Rosalie's heart was heavy as she stepped down on to the path. Her courage waning, she wanted to turn and run. Then the door opened suddenly; a young girl stood there. She stared with astonishment at the well-dressed lady in front of her, then gave a rather unsteady curtsy.

Rosalie gulped back the lump in her throat. 'Good day,' she said, feeling embarrassed. 'To whom am I speaking?'

'Sophie, Sophie Pendeen,' the girl answered nervously.

Rosalie sighed with audible relief, then she smiled to herself at her own stupidity. For a fleeting second she had thought that Michael had a wife. She saw now the same dark curls and shining eyes. This was Michael's eighteen-year-old sister who had been away at their eldest brother Matthew's when Rosalie had stayed at the farm. The one whose dress she had borrowed.

'Is Michael—?' She hesitated. 'Tom, or your mother at home?' she asked.

The girl nodded, then vanished quickly inside.

Mary Pendeen came to the door, her hands covered in flour from kneading dough. She looked at Rosalie with amazement, then gave a quick bob.

'Good day, Mistress. What can I do for 'ee?'

Rosalie bit her lip. Michael's mother did not recognise her.

'It is Rosalie, Mistress Pendeen,' she said.

Mary Pendeen's eyes searched the young face in front of her, then, as recognition dawned, they lit up with joy.

'Rosalie!' she exclaimed, wiping her own hands hurriedly on her apron before clasping Rosalie's hands. 'You'm come to see Michael?' Then her face clouded. 'He's not yere, m'dear, but come in, come in.' She led the way inside, glancing continually at Rosalie's elegantly cut green riding habit, shaking her head incredulously. 'I knowed you'm no peasant maid,' she said. 'But I didna' dream you'm such a fine lady.' She put the black kettle over the fire, indicating to Rosalie to sit down at the table. Then she sat down herself and her eyes filled with tears.

''Twould have to be Michael,' she whispered sadly, brushing the tears away with embarrassment. ''Twould have to be Michael fell in love wi' a lady.' She shook her head slowly. 'Always the one wi' the fine ideas; readin' so much. Dreamin' of a ship of his own, an' I don't know what else.' She looked at Rosalie as if trying to read her mind. The smell of warm cake wafted in from the kitchen.

'Lors a me!' she exclaimed. 'Forgettin' me bakin', I be.' She bustled off, leaving Rosalie to let her eyes roam around the room. It had not changed. The same white walls, the black-painted beams, the model boat that Michael had whittled from a piece of yew. A loud banging on the front door brought Mary Pendeen hurrying through to answer it.

''Tis the steward, the Trevia steward for the

dues,' she called over her shoulder.

Rosalie stared after her. Did Sir Hugh Trevia own the Pendeens' farm, too? Michael had never mentioned it. Realising that he might recognise her, she made a hasty retreat into the kitchen. She stood by the window, watching two hens flying at each other in a squabble.

'So you've come back, Mistress Harvey. If 'tis more fun you're wanting, then Michael's away.'

Rosalie turned, startled, shocked by the cynical voice from the open doorway. Tom Pendeen stood there, so like his elder brother, except for his height and the three years between them. She stared at him in disbelief, the courage that his mother's greeting had given her fading into unsurety. When Tom had taken her back to Trevia he had been kind, understanding. Why these harsh words now?

He came into the kitchen, his sheepdog close on his heels. He crossed to the soft water pump and swilled his hands and face. 'Michael's away,' he repeated when he had dried. He regarded Rosalie with a frowning face. 'Too busy to come here, to take you on outings to amuse you.'

Rosalie did not speak; she just stared at Tom, hardly believing her ears. Was that how Michael had seen it? Could he possibly have been 'just amusing' her? Had it all been a joke when he told her he loved her?

A man's raised voice came to them through the closed living-room door.

Tom looked up in surprise. 'Is the steward here?' he asked.

She nodded. 'Yes.'

Tom turned towards the door, but stopped with his hand on the latch.

'Michael's doing fine now, Rosalie. He's scores of men he can call on to work for him.' The pride in his voice changed to almost a pleading. 'Don't mix him up again.' He was not against her. He just thought her bad for Michael. That was all that mattered. He opened the door quickly and was gone. Rosalie looked after him numbly. It seemed he had closed the door on her life.

The door to the dairy was open as she passed on her hurried way out. Sophie was there, methodically turning the butter churn. Rosalie stopped for a moment, watching. Her long shadow fell across the stone floor. Sophie saw it and looked up. She stopped her turning, hesitated for a second, then came to the door.

'You're Rosalie,' she said, eagerness showing in her voice. 'Michael's Rosalie.'

Rosalie managed a smile as she nodded.

'Are you going to Padstow?' the girl asked.

'Is Michael at Padstow?' The question almost died on her lips. Sophie would be in trouble with Tom for disclosing the fact.

Sophie nodded. 'Did Mother not tell 'ee?'

Rosalie bit her lip, then the truth came to her

aid. 'The steward from Trevia came. I had to leave. Is Michael staying with your aunt?' She held her breath, dreading that Tom would come.

'Aye.' Sophie's eyes shone with pride. 'Michael's his own smuggling ring now,' she said. 'He's fifty men to do the riding, an' boats he contracts to do the runs.'

So that was what Tom had meant. Rosalie understood now. She glanced back at the kitchen door, but she saw only the hens scratching in the mud.

'Can I get back to my horse without the steward seeing me from the window?' she asked.

Sophie nodded and led the way round the house.

Rosalie smiled and waved as she rode away, yet her heart was still as heavy as when she had come. Who was she to believe? Surely Michael would be more likely to confide in Tom. She wondered what his mother would have said had she heard Tom's words. Did she, too, think Michael was better off not seeing Rosalie again?

CHAPTER FOURTEEN

'Single room?' The landlord of the White Hart at Padstow eyed the girl standing by his reception desk with suspicion. She looked well fed, even clean, but he disliked peasant girls taking rooms at his inn. This one was even more dubious than the last one he had let a room to. She had a peculiar accent, too. He was unable to place it.

'Single room?' he repeated, walking slowly around the desk to take a look at the baggage she had brought on the stage.

Rosalie ran her hands nervously down her skirts. She had made a green dress of local cloth whilst she had been at Trevia. She regarded the landlord's frowning face with bafflement. Why was he reluctant to let her have a room?

'Can 'ee pay?' he demanded at last.

Mistress Harvey just stifled her indignation in time. 'I will pay two nights in advance,' she said, managing to keep her voice calm.

The landlord leaned over the desk without answering her. He turned the pages of the register slowly, took up a quill, and looked up at Rosalie with narrowed eyes. 'Name?' he asked.

Rosalie hesitated, just for a second. She remembered Michael saying he had only heard her name in France before.

'Rose Harvey,' she said boldly.

The man wrote it down, then held out his hand for the money. 'Room sixteen, on the top floor,' he said, waving his hand towards the stairs. He made no move to assist her with her baggage, or to summon anyone to do so. Rosalie picked up the two bags and walked towards the stairs.

'Mind, we keep a respectable house yere,' he called after her.

Her colour heightened with anger, but she checked the curt reply on her lips. She almost wished now she had taken a room at the George and Dragon. Yet the likelihood of encountering one of the Tregars was too great.

She inspected the room, reminding herself that she was not travelling as Mistress Harvey who would have caused a scene at its size and debatable cleanliness. She opened the window wide to let in some air. She then took a walk in the town, making her way warily towards the harbour.

Her fair hair was put up into a white cap. If she met any of the Tregars, she could turn her face away in time. There were several boats in the harbour; not one of them looked like the bare wooden shell she had seen in the shipyard those months before. She stepped carefully over the nets and ropes that cluttered the quay. Would she recognise Michael's boat even if it was there?

She read the name of each one as she passed. The *Wanderer*, *St Izzy*. The tide was going out. The larger boats, only just supported by the water, were beginning to list over on to their keel supports.

She came to what she later knew to be a

two-masted lugger; then she stopped. The colour drained from her cheeks; her pulse quickened as she stared at the name. Painted in blue letters she saw her own name, *Rosalie*, on the bows. Beneath, in neat black letters, was her owner, Michael Pendeen.

When the first shock had subsided, she glanced self-consciously around the quay. No one was watching; the few people there were too busy with some task or another.

Rosalie walked alongside the boat, looking down on to her sloping deck. Nets, folded neatly. A pile of coiled ropes. A dozen or so lobster pots. Two rafts, one lashed to each mast. The boat seemed prepared for a fishing trip. Was Michael sailing on the next tide? She remembered his explaining the importance of catching the tide right. The harbour, just inside the estuary of the River Camel, was affected not only by the tide but also by the flow of the river. She sauntered unhurriedly towards a group of fishermen a short distance away.

'Could you oblige me with the time of the next high tide, please?' she asked.

When the answer was given, she thanked them politely, then went back to her room at the White Hart.

Rosalie retired to bed early that night, partly because she wanted to preclude any possible meeting with the Tregar men; mostly because she intended to go down to the quay before three in the morning.

The night sky was black; moonless. Sparkling diamonds glittered across it, but gave no light to the earth, as Rosalie trod cautiously back to the quay. She tripped over a snoring figure sprawled on the cobblestones, almost falling flat on her face. Two faceless, laughing men caught her between them as she turned a corner. She wriggled free as they swayed drunkenly. She ran like a hare. The harbour was lit by only three lamps, throwing barely enough light for her to see the difference between the water and the quay. Except that the quay was a dark, still mass, whereas the water moved, shimmered and splashed noisily.

The tide was already high when she reached Michael's lugger, the deck level with the jetty. She stood back in the shadows, leaning wearily against the wall of a nearby fisherman's cottage. She had given Michael an hour. An hour before she had concluded he would sail. Surely he would come early, there would be time for them to talk before he left. The time dragged painfully slowly. She found herself sinking to the floor, resting on her haunches. Soon her head began to nod.

She woke suddenly, panicked, and rushed to the side of the quay. The *Rosalie* was still rising with the tide, still unoccupied. Supposing she fell asleep again, and Michael came. He could take the boat out of the harbour without even knowing she was there. She stared for a moment at the swaying lugger. Then quickly, she walked back to the cottage wall. After a brief glance around, she lifted her skirts high; then she ran straight for the boat and jumped. She landed bruised and terrified. But she landed on the deck.

An oilskin cover was folded in the stern, covering a pile of blankets. She wriggled herself inside them and pulled the cover over her head. Now she would be bound to hear the men arrive. She sighed with relief. In only a short time she grew accustomed to the gentle rising and falling of the craft. She closed her eyes, sure now that Michael could not sail without seeing her, safe from any stray drunkards on the quay. Her eyes closed, and the tenseness of her body slowly melted away.

When Rosalie awoke, the movement had increased to a severe rolling from side to side. She lay still, listening. The boat lifted suddenly, then dipped with a loud thud into the water. Spring tides! ... Flooding! ... The memories of winter gales rushed into her mind. Frantically, she threw back the cover and thrust out her head.

The man with his hand on the tiller let go of it in surprise as the white cap suddenly appeared beside him in the darkness. He grabbed the wooden bar just in time as the lugger began to turn. Rosalie stared up at the large white sail billowing above her, realising with bewilderment that they were at sea, that the men had boarded the boat, hoisted the sails and still she had slept on.

'George, there be a maid yere,' a voice boomed beside her.

She pulled herself out on to the deck and stood up. The boat took another dive. She found herself lying down again, this time not of her own choice. A strong arm helped her up; sat her down on the plank seat at the side of the boat. Then George lit a lantern and she could see him. He was around forty, with a large nose and black-bearded chin. He eyed her from head to foot before speaking.

'Well! What've 'ee to say?' he growled ill-humouredly.

Rosalie tried to look past him into the blackness. She had heard another voice. Why did Michael not come? The lantern made her squint as she looked up into the enquiring, frowning eyes.

'I would like to speak to Mr Pendeen,' she said, trying to sound dignified despite her undignified entrance.

George's eyes opened wider. His thick black eyebrows shot up. 'The Capt'n!' he bellowed. 'Did 'ee think Michael be yere?'

Rosalie straightened her shoulders, lifted her chin. 'Certainly. I wished to see him.'

'What be your name, girl?' the man at the tiller demanded, leaning towards her.

She said nothing. She might as well say, 'My name's on the bow of this boat.'

The man who was still aft called back to

them. It was not Michael's voice.

'What's amiss, George?'

'There be a maid yere, says her wants to see Michael.' The lantern just reached another face peering round the mizzen sail.

'Be she that cousin of 'ee? Tregar's daughter. The one 'ee—'

'I am not Emma Tregar.' Rosalie did not let him finish, though she immediately wished she had.

'But you know 'ee,' George said, scratching his head. There was a long silence, then he went on, 'Well, the Capt'n'll be right mad wi' 'ee, I'll wager. Like as not 'ee'll put 'ee off on they rocks.'

Whatever Michael did, she doubted he would do that. He could not have changed so much. But where was he?

George heaved an almighty sigh and snuffed out the lantern.

'You best sit yere an' 'old on till we picked up the Capt'n,' he said.

'You are picking up Michael?' Rosalie's voice found its full volume at last.

'Aye, in ten minutes or so, but I'm damned if I know what 'ee'll say. We can't take 'ee wi' us, that's for certain sure.' He climbed back aft and she heard him grumbling to his companion there.

She held on firmly to the side, her eyes getting more accustomed to the darkness. She wished she had brought her cloak. The night air on the quay had been warm. She had not intended to be sailing the seas. The breeze was cool and the sea sprayed her with every heavy pitch. The man at the tiller was silent, standing with his eyes glued ahead.

Suddenly, George appeared again. He began lowering the mizzen sail, leaving only the trysail set. Rosalie leaned precariously over the side. She saw nothing but blackness, heard nothing but the splash of the waves. Then in the distance she saw a tiny pinhead of light. She knew it was Michael. Her courage grew fainter, her doubts returned. Would he really be angry? Impulsively, she pulled the pins that held her cap, letting her hair fall over her shoulders as he had always seen it.

Michael handed his lantern across before he climbed from the rocks. Rosalie saw only the tall, slim shape, but she knew it was him. How she wished they could have been alone when they met. Why did it have to be in the company of three strange men?

'We've a problem for 'ee, Capt'n.' George wasted no time. 'There be a maid astern says she knows 'ee.'

'A maid!' Michael's voice showed no pleasure at the prospect. 'What the bloody hell d'you let a *maid* on board for?'

'We didna' rightly know, Michael. She was hid in they blankets.'

Michael's form came across the boat towards Rosalie. She sat speechless, staring up at him.

'Pass the lantern, George. I can't see her.'

The lantern was swung over and its light swung across her face.

'Rosalie!' Michael's voice vibrated with surprise. He dropped to his knees at her feet, saying her name again. This time she heard joy in his voice; not anger, not disapproval, but undisguised joy. He leaned beside her and hung the lantern on an iron hook. Then he took her face in his hands, completely oblivious to the three pairs of watching eyes behind him. He felt the coldness of her cheeks; turned quickly to the man at the tiller.

'Have you no sense, Jack?' he said. 'Throw blankets over, will you?'

Rosalie had a blanket wrapped round her shoulders; another was put across her knees. Michael sat on the seat beside her.

'Are we sailing?' he shouted to the three dumbfounded men. 'Or are we anchored here till dawn?'

George leaned towards him, his thick eyebrows joining in the middle of his perplexed face. 'But, Capt'n,' he gasped, 'we'm not taking the maid with we. You'd not take a maid moonlighting?'

Michael leaned back on to the gunwale, putting a firm arm around Rosalie's shoulders. 'I'd take this one anywhere,' he said, pride in his voice. 'This is Mistress Harvey. Mistress Rosalie Harvey.'

George looked at Rosalie, then back to Michael. He did not speak. He had always thought it an odd name for Michael to choose for his boat. It was suddenly clear. He gave the man who was still nameless a push.

'Anchor!' he growled, as he hoisted the mizzen sail.

Michael waited until they were well underway before he turned Rosalie's face gently towards him.

'Why did you come back?' he asked quietly, knowing the answer, yet needing to hear her say it.

She was perfectly aware that she could say she came back for news of the boys, but there seemed no reason to lie.

'I came back to you,' she whispered. 'If you want me.'

Michael shook his head slowly, as if he still could not believe his own eyes. 'If I want you,' he said, his voice breaking with emotion. 'I've wanted you every hour, every minute since you left.'

The boat took a sudden dive, throwing her hard against him. She stayed there, held close in his arms as he kissed her, completely heedless of the cold salt spray that covered them.

* * *

When Rosalie woke for the second time on

Michael's lugger it was long past dawn. He had made a bed for her on the mizzen raft. She had lain awake for some time looking up at the stars, but eventually weariness had closed her eyes.

'You'd best eat before you get up, Rosalie,' Michael's voice said beside her. He handed her a pile of neatly cut sandwiches wrapped in a white cloth. Then he grinned and sat down at her side. 'Emma cut those,' he said. 'I've a mind she'd be greatly pleased 'tis you eating them.'

'Did you think I was Emma last night?' she asked.

Michael laughed. 'Aye, for a while. I'd've given her a piece of my mind if 'twas she. I'll not have meddling girls on my boat.'

Rosalie ate a cheese sandwich hungrily. Michael handed her a flask.

''Tis only ale, my love. You'll not like it, but 'twill stay your thirst awhile.'

She put the flask to her mouth, glad of anything to wet her lips. She looked up at him and smiled to herself. He had not changed. His dark eyes still shone when he smiled. His weathered, angular face, still as handsome. Tom had been wrong, so very wrong. Michael still had time for her. She leaned her head back lazily; gazed up at the bright blue sky of morning, at the wind-filled sails that took them forward.

'Where are we going?' she asked, quite unconcerned.

'To Guernsey, my love. We've a cargo of spirits to smuggle back for the merchants of Lans'n.'

He held out his hand and pulled her to her feet, steadying her until she was sitting safely in the bows. The wind was due west. They were making good time under a clear sky.

George's voice carried to Michael with urgency in its tone. 'Cutter to starboard, Capt'n.'

Michael's eyes scanned the sea. 'We'll fish,' he called back. 'There's a patch of seagulls, sou'-sou'-west, Jack.'

The boat began turning. Michael lowered the foresail as George and the man whose name Rosalie had discovered was Silas held the net in readiness on the port side. Rosalie furrowed her brow. Why did they suddenly have to fish?

Michael saw her frown. He came back to her just as the net hit the water.

'The ship yonder,' he explained, waving his arm to the west. ''Tis a revenue cutter. We're a fishing boat, so we must fish.'

'But why near the seagulls?'

He laughed. 'Where there's seagulls there's fish,' he said.

The catch was a good one. Rosalie watched as the jumping, squirming mackerel were landed; their shining bodies becoming suddenly still, their eyes suddenly dull. When the hatch was opened they slid lifelessly down into the falsely lined hold.

Soon, the revenue cutter was gliding smoothly over the horizon. The *Rosalie*'s anchor was weighed, her sails hoisted. Her captain took the tiller and turned her southeastwards to the Channel Islands.

He was worried that Rosalie was with them. There was always danger at sea; that danger ten times worse when you sailed in a smuggler's boat. When he had found her on board he had considered immediately taking the lugger back to Padstow, but this run was important. He was meeting the agent at L'Ancresse to arrange for the next month's cargoes. And now that Rosalie was back, he needed those cargoes.

He watched her face held up to the skies, her long hair blown by the warm breeze. He had hardly dared to hope that she would come back. Yet he had known that if she did return, she would have come to stay. He had set up the smuggling ring with that knowledge. It was the only way he could earn more money. His careful planning was paying off well. He had enough money for another boat already. Yet perchance he would be buying a house instead. He smiled to himself. Always the optimist, he mused. He was not that sure of her. She would see the way he earned his living today—that was a good thing. He could never hide anything from her. She must know the plain, undisguised truth. There could be problems ahead even he had not thought of, and the

Lord knows he had thought of enough. He considered this run as safe as any. The weather was good, although a squall could blow up anytime. He was a little surprised that Rosalie had shown no signs of seasickness, this being her first time at sea. She had taken to it like a time-served tar. He smiled; she probably had never heard of seasickness. He wondered if her brothers had done as well.

As Michael had hoped, the run was smooth, the weather held, and the cargo was got on board with little difficulty. He went on shore on Guernsey, cutting his stay to a minimum as he arranged the dates and times for future runs for the *Rosalie* and the six other boats he contracted regularly.

It was well before dawn on the following day when they sailed back through the Celtic Sea towards Michael's own private landing place. Rosalie had quite enjoyed the trip. She had felt no nervousness of the sea. George had promised to collect her bags from the White Hart when he reached Padstow. She secretly wondered what the landlord had made of her absence. He had obviously considered her a loose woman.

The lugger headed towards the pale glimmer of a welcoming lantern. As they neared the coast Rosalie saw it lit the entrance of a small cave—a cave that had no beach, with only sheer cliff above it and a cluster of rocks at its narrow mouth. The sails were furled; the anchor dragging as the *Rosalie* hoved to. Michael sprang quickly on to the rocks with a line, lashing it around a large boulder.

'Stay aboard till we've the cargo landed,' he called to Rosalie in a low voice.

The men began unloading the kegs from the concealed hatch to the main hold, passing them from one to another. Rosalie remembered with a smile the last time she had watched a cargo unloaded; that fateful night when Michael had caught her on the cliffs. How different she felt now. How long ago it seemed, yet her brothers had still not returned.

She watched with astonishment as Michael lifted each keg, placing it in a narrow, horizontal gap before turning to accept the next. She strained her eyes in the dim light; the kegs seemed to vanish as he put them in. Fifty kegs disappeared into the darkness.

George, already in receipt of his instructions from Michael, came over to Rosalie and helped her to her feet. Then, to her surprise, he picked her suddenly up in his arms, held her for a moment whilst Jack steadied the swaying lugger, then handed her over to Michael's waiting arms.

When Michael let her feet slip gently on to the rocks, she clung to him fearfully, quite sure that the granite at her feet was endeavouring to throw her into the black water. After a few minutes her body became accustomed again to the stationary existence of land. It was only the boat that was moving, and its three occupants stood shaking with silent laughter at her balancing act.

Michael untied the line and tossed it over.

'Mind you've a good catch when you make harbour,' he called as the *Rosalie* slipped silently out to sea.

Rosalie looked around her apprehensively. They seemed completely marooned. Certainly no way upwards. She looked at Michael hopefully.

'We've to go through the cave,' he said.

She shivered a little. She was not cold, but caves were not her favourite places. This one was no different when she squeezed through its narrow entrance. She doubted anyone fatter would get through at all. She was intrigued to know what happened to the vanishing kegs. When the circle of light from Michael's lantern reached the side of the cave, she understood. How ingenious, she thought. The rocks had been cut to form a smooth slope down to the back of the cave. As each keg had been pushed through the slit, it had rolled gently down on to what looked like a low, four-wheeled wooden cart. Michael set each one on end to make them more stable.

'Where do we come out?' she asked. She could see nothing that looked like an opening.

'On the cliff top,' he answered, coming back to her. 'This cave leads into an old tin mine. We've to go up the shaft.'

She shuddered, then felt his arm around her.

'You'll not need to come here again,' he said, sounding concerned. 'But I'd a mind you'd sooner come with me than go back to Padstow. I've to come here tonight and we'll ride these beauties into Lans'n.'

They made their way down a narrow tunnel. Even Rosalie had to bend her back; Michael was bent almost double in places. A rope ran the length on the ground beside them. Cut into the rocky floor were channels for the wheels of the cart.

Eventually, Rosalie felt a cold draught of air; she saw a glimmer of daylight above them. They had reached the shaft. Michael pulled hard on rope at his feet. A loud rumbling sound echoed through the mine. Rosalie went stiff with terror. Then slowly she relaxed as the noise came nearer and she realised it was the cart, set in motion by Michael's pull on the rope. It brought the kegs of spirit to the bottom of the shaft to await their removal when darkness fell again.

Dawn was past. They shielded their eyes against the pale gold of day, as they climbed into the tiny ruin of the wheelhouse. The freshness of the air filled their lungs after the dank seaweed odour of the cave and mine. Michael heaved up the rope ladder. Then pulling a stone from the wall, he wedged the ladder behind it, then replaced the stone. His eyes, now more accustomed to the light, scanned the clifftop from the doorway. Above the ground level only the birds moved.

Sea pinks and fern stretched ahead of them as they stepped out hand in hand on the six-mile walk to the Pendeens' farm. Celandine and violets leaned their frail heads against the tall grasses. Across the valley the wind rippled over the young green corn as a hand stroked gently through velvet.

For Rosalie, the world was beautiful again. They had talked only of the past months; of the mill's failure, of the school that Rosalie had started, and of the forthcoming sale of her home and its contents. The return of her brothers was as far into the future as they ventured.

As they walked Michael began singing, as he often did.

> My sweetheart, come along.
> Don't you hear the fond song,
> The sweet notes of the nightingale flow?
> Don't you hear the fond tale of the sweet nightingale
> as she sings in the valley below...?

There were no nightingales, only seagulls and curlews, but as he reached the fourth verse they were striding down a lane with its stone hedges carpeted in primroses. Rosalie joined in and sang:

Pray sit yourself down,
with me on the ground,
On this bank where the primroses grow.
You shall hear the fond tale of the sweet
  nightingale
as she sings in the valley below...

They did not sing the last verse. They both knew the words, but they were not quite ready for them yet.

CHAPTER FIFTEEN

As Tom Pendeen drove the cows down into the yard, he started laughing. It was something he had done quite often in the last two weeks. He had once again noticed Rosalie running across the yard, diving into the house just in time as the first of the cows ambled towards her. Despite continual reassurances from both Michael and Tom, she was still unable to meet the cows face to face. She could catch, groom, saddle and ride any horse; but meeting cows was different.

She had been nervous of meeting Tom when she had walked down into the valley on that fine late May morning. Tom, however, had received her courteously. He had even echoed Michael's suggestion that she bring her trunk from Trevia and stay at the farm.

'You'll be thinking my manners bad,' he had said on the first occasion that they were alone. 'I mistook your intentions. I'm sorry.' Then he had grinned. ''Tis most likely Michael knew you better than I,' he said.

She had smiled with him then. Since, they had been the best of friends.

Rosalie had just visited the henhouse when the cows had appeared around the corner. She had been in most of the day, offering to fetch the eggs for a breath of fresh air. Life on the farm was still strange to her, yet she much preferred it to staying at Trevia. There was a closeness in this Pendeen family into which she had been taken without question. No one expected her to do farm work, yet she was given the same treatment as if she had done it. She missed the fine Arabs at home and at Trevia, but Michael had had a saddle made for her and she rode any of the Pendeens' moorland ponies that were not wanted. She had noticed that both Michael and Tom used saddles now.

Michael was away at Launceston bargaining with the merchants for the price of the goods he had delivered to them. He also took orders for the next cargoes to be landed. Rosalie had learned quickly and well about the art of smuggling. The need for absolute secrecy of every cargo. The importance that no one knew that Michael Pendeen, the agent, was in fact only working for himself. That the decisions he took away to ask his imaginary employer were already made before he left the room.

Rosalie sighed as she carefully placed the eggs next to Mary Pendeen's bowl of rising dough. Michael had promised he would spend more time at the farm in the next week. The shearing was to be done; soon the hay would need cutting. He always allowed days to help Tom at times like these. She was as impatient for his return as always. Yet she had not been idle whilst he was away.

She returned to the living-room, sat down at the table and took up a quill. She had always been good at figures, and she wrote now in a neat hand.

	£	s	d
Five hundredweight of tea cost	79	0	0
Eighty half-ankers of brandy cost	40	0	0
Payment to riders (20 men at 6s)	6	0	0
Payment to ship's crew (4 men at 25s)	5	0	0
Payment farmers, loan horses and carts (30 × 3d)		7	6
Payment to John Wearne to light mine lantern		1	6
One half-anker of brandy for men		10	0
Total	130	19	0

	£	s	d
Sale of tea	140	0	0

Sale of brandy	80	0	0
Total	220	0	0
Subtract expenses	130	19	0
Profit	89	1	0

Unlike most of his contemporaries, Michael always asked before he borrowed, and he paid well.

Mistress Pendeen sat rocking slowly in her chair near the window, thinking of the four sons she had raised, three of them content to farm as their father had done. Even the one daughter who had survived was walking out with a farmer's son. But not Michael. How he'd met this daughter of a gentleman she didn't know. When she'd asked him, he'd laughed. 'I found her on the cliffs in the moonlight,' he'd said. She'd told him to stop his teasing, but he'd not change the tale. She saw why he'd fallen for she. She was real pretty. Clever, too; like Michael. When they talked together, they talked of books, of plays; of things she, his mother, never knew the like. No peasant wench would've suited Michael. He'd always been one for a pretty face. Always in demand at the barn dance they had when the harvest was cut. There wasn't a wench in Camelford didn't know Michael Pendeen. But he'd not've wed any of they.

The kettle sang and hissed on the fire. She stopped rocking and went over to pour the boiling water on the tea in the pot. Never be short of tea, she thought. Not with Michael bringing it in in oilskins from France. He'll wed she. Though the Lord knows where they'll live. She sighed. Used to servants, was she. Never made so much as a mutton stew in her life, though she sews well enough.

Hoofbeats, coming nearer. Two heads raised to listen, then a quick glance at each other and a smile. Rosalie closed the book carefully, placing it in the hiding place beneath the flagstones as Michael had shown her. Then she ran into the kitchen to watch from the window.

Mary Pendeen smiled to herself. She was always glad to hear Michael arrive. She always feared his arrest on land; his drowning at sea. Likely he'd be less reckless now. She latched the kitchen door, sat down and began rocking again.

Michael reined his grey as he saw the cows. He walked him slowly through them, then dismounted by the stable door, leading the pony inside. Rosalie stared at the cows with annoyance. If they were not there she would have run across the yard to him. She opened the door slightly and stood waiting. He would unsaddle and rub down his horse first. When Michael emerged a full fifteen minutes later Rosalie's eyes widened in surprise. He was leading the bay colt she often rode and Tom's black mare. Both were saddled. Was he riding out again? But Tom was still busy milking. There were still five cows in the yard.

She opened the door wider, calling across to him. He turned his head, saw her and smiled. He took the ponies round to the front of the house, tethered them to the fence, then came back and into the kitchen.

'You're rising brave,' he laughed, picking her up and swinging her round. 'The door wide open; the cows in the yard. You'll have them fancying a cup of tea.'

'Put me down, Michael,' she begged in a whisper. 'Your mother's in there.'

He let her down gently, but still held her in his arms.

'Am I to keep my distance and greet you with polite conversation?' he said as he kissed her.

'Where are you riding?' she asked as soon as she was able.

'Where are *we* riding?' he corrected. 'I've something to show you. Go and change into your riding clothes whilst I take a bite to eat.'

She obeyed without question, still puzzled. What could he want to show her that was so urgent? He was helping himself to gooseberry pie and his mother was pouring him a second cup of tea when Rosalie came down. He got to his feet, drinking his tea standing up.

'We'll be back before dark, Mother,' he said.

'Where are we going?' Rosalie asked impatiently.

Michael did not answer, he just grinned at her over his cup. He was obviously pleased about something, so she did not persist with the question.

Rosalie was mounted first, as Michael called in to see Tom before he joined her. They rode away from the farm at a trot, heading towards the coast.

Michael's face had lost its secretive smile. He glanced across at Rosalie anxiously as if he had sudden doubts about what he was doing. When they had ridden two miles he reined his mount suddenly. Rosalie did the same.

'I've something to say before we go further,' he said slowly. 'Shall we walk awhile?'

Rosalie dismounted without waiting for his help. Michael loosed the ponies to graze; then, taking Rosalie's hand, he crossed to a field gate and leaned on the top bar.

They gazed together over the valley. The patchwork rectangles of corn, peas, mowing grass; now and then a field of yellow mustard; cows and sheep grazing in another; scarlet poppies already dotted amongst the corn in the fore. A buzzard circled over their heads, his keen eyes watching their movements; then suddenly, with a few skilful strokes of his wings, he soared over the valley to be lost in a dense wooded slope. The sun, slowly nearing the west, glowed gold in a crimson sky. Everywhere, the trees of June were bursting green; heavy with blossom, alive with bees and butterflies.

Michael turned to Rosalie, solemn.

'We've had little talk of the future, Rosalie,' he said gently, 'yet it stretches before us like the hills over yonder. Aye, and with as many glorious peaks, as many bad pitholes, as any journey we could take.'

He hesitated, then squeezed her hand as if to give himself courage. 'Will you make that journey at my side, Rosalie? Will you be my wife?'

He saw the answer he wanted, shining from her blue eyes. Then she nodded, the words somehow gone from her lips.

He gripped her shoulders and just looked down at her for a full minute before he kissed her. Then he held her to him and stood speechless as if so much joy was too much to bear.

Suddenly, the mysterious gleam returned to his eyes; he glanced up at the sky, saying hurriedly, 'We must ride. The day's too near close. I've so much to show you.'

Rosalie shook her head, laughing. Then they ran, caught their ponies, and mounted quickly.

They had ridden barely half a mile when they reached a small copse set with sprawling oaks and tall horse-chestnuts. As they wended their way through the trees Michael called across to her:

'I've arranged new cargoes for the *Rosalie*.'

'But why?'

'I'll have her do no more smuggling with your name on her bows,' he declared.

'But what will happen to the ones ...?'

'We've a new ship on contract now. She'll take over from next Saturday. And I'll not go myself once we're wed.'

Everything planned. Always guarding her safety. She knew how much he enjoyed those moonlight runs, the danger. Yet he would give them up for her.

'We'll still bring in the same cargoes,' he went on. ''Twill make little difference to the money.'

Rosalie smiled at the mention of money. Michael had been surprised when she had told him about the mill. Yet he had seemed almost pleased. She had very little of her own money left now. There would be some over from debts after the sale of the house. Had she gone back to Nottingham, she would certainly have needed that allowance from Robert...Robert! She hardly ever thought of him now. It was barely six weeks since she had left him in London, yet it seemed like a year.

They came to the end of the copse; to a wide garden gate that hung crooked on its hinges. On horseback they could see over the holly hedge. Rosalie stared in amazement. Michael was dismounting and tethering his horse. She looked again over the hedge, at the long, low-roofed house that stood there. Was this what Michael wanted to show her?

'Tis ours—if you like it,' he said, as she followed him through the gate. 'There's much needs to be done, but 'twould not take long with a couple of good men.'

He took a large iron key from his pocket and opened the door. The garden they had walked through was completely wild. Yet, they had bent low beneath lilac, heavy with purple flowers. The slate path was edged with the deep pink of the tamarisk. And between the tall nettles she had seen roses; yellow, crimson. She had smelled their fragrance as she passed.

'Tis sound and dry.' Michael's words brought her thoughts from the garden. 'I've a mind 'twill be big enough. There's room for your brothers. I was none too sure how many servants we'll need. You've more knowledge of that than I.'

The dust was thick everywhere, shown up by the sunlight that streamed through the windows. There were footprints already ahead of them as Michael showed her first the kitchen; the dining-room, the stairs to the servants' rooms.

He saw her looking at the footprints; leaned towards her and grinned. 'I was here this morning,' he said. ''Twas the hardest thing I've done, not to come to the farm to see you. But I'd still to ride back to Lans'n.'

His mouth jerked open, remembering. ''Twas a cargo of fine silks landed last night. I've put some aside for you.'

'Thank you.'

The rooms were not large. At least to Rosalie they were not large, but she liked this house. Even at this late hour of day, it was light; it felt a friendly house. She could see why Michael liked it; but could he really afford a house like this? When she had thought of marrying him, she had thought of living at the farm. When she told him, he burst out laughing.

'With the cows!' he exclaimed. 'If I'd no house to offer you, I'd not have asked you to wed me, my love. There'd be no room at the farm with Tom being wed after the harvest.'

'Tom!'

'Aye, did he not tell you? He's to wed Jenny Trenear, the saddler's daughter. She's a likeable enough girl, though she'd not hold a candle to you.' He ran his fingers through her hair, sighing. 'But then, there's no woman living who ever will, leastways not for me.'

They were upstairs in the bedroom admiring the view to the sea. Michael brushed the cobwebs from the window to push it open. He had to bang it hard before it would move. Then, when it opened, the fragrance from the jungle that was the garden came floating in. A blackbird, perched on a damson tree under the window, vibrated his song through the evening air.

Rosalie gazed out over the wilderness, picturing it with the lawns cut, with the roses pruned, with the weeds pulled.

'I'll walk in this garden with you, Michael Pendeen,' she said. 'With my head in the air and my arm through yours. And I shall be proud to be mistress of—' She stopped and turned to him. 'Has it a name, Michael?' she said.

'Lowarth Tek,' he answered, then he laughed. ''Tis hardly suitable now.'

'What does it mean?'

'Oh—beautiful garden.' He glanced out of the window again. 'I'd thought a man and his wife to start with. Mansel Polruan's the man for any garden, and his wife's a good cook. Would they manage a house like this, to start with anyway?' he asked anxiously.

'I'm sure they would. I had not expected servants at all.'

They went down the stairs into the parlour. It was a good-sized room with large mullioned windows.

'This room must be you,' Michael said slowly. 'We'll have a fine carpet, velvet curtains at the windows.'

'And in here I shall wear elegant gowns for you,' she hesitated, 'or would you think that wrong, Michael?'

'You'll wear what you choose, my love.' He laughed and came over to her. 'Must I wear my hair in a velvet bow and wear silver buckles on my shoes?'

She put up her hands, pushed back his hair

and held it there. 'It would suit you well,' she laughed. Then she let it go and pulled a face. 'But I prefer it how you wear it. I would not have you changed, Michael. For I'll wed you as you are. If I can make our home with a little more comfort than you are used to, then I'll do it. But I shall not miss the life I leave behind, nor the place in society it gave me; for in you I gain so much more.'

He pulled her to him then; locked her in his arms and kissed her. She had come back to him without even knowing about his good earnings from the smuggling ring.

''Tis a strange trick of fate,' he said. 'The mill going broke. There'll be those who'll say I've wed you for your money. Yet, though 'tis not true, we must not tell them about the mill. We must not stop the gossip.' He let her go and raised his hands in despair. ''Twould be better for my pride to have it known 'twas I bought the house. But then there'd be those'd want to know where I got the money.' He sighed. 'So I'll be content that those who matter know the truth.' He shrugged his shoulders and went to the window. 'Those who don't matter can say what they please.'

She saw sadness in his eyes, just for a moment, then he smiled again. They stood in silence; a silence of unspoken words that did not need to be said. For Michael knew that she understood.

She went to him, putting her arm through

his.

'The drapes,' she said. 'I've an idea. Could I not bring those from Charlesworth Hall? Some of them are almost new. They do not need to be sold.'

'Have anything you wish, my love, but mind the stage can't carry too much.'

She bit her lip and was silent.

'What is it?' he asked with humour. 'I doubt it could carry your pianoforte.'

'No, it is not that. There's one thing I would like.'

'Then name it. I'm intrigued.'

'A servant. One who has been with me all my life. She would need no wages, just a home. She could teach me more about running a house. I've been dreading turning her—' She did not finish.

'Then she must come. If you write to her, she could pack the things you need and bring them on the coach. Write tomorrow, tell her to come straight away. She could stay with James and Meg till the house is ready.'

Rosalie beamed. She spun away from him, dancing around the room.

'Oh, Michael!' she cried. 'I do like this house.'

'Then I did right to buy it without asking you first?'

'You've bought it already?'

'Aye, this very morn. I wanted a house near enough the farm, for the times when I'm away.'

He opened a narrow door that went off the parlour. 'Would you think me foolish if I made this a library?'

Rosalie peered into the room. It was small. Much smaller than any library that she had seen; but with its walls lined with shelves it would make a good library. She told Michael so, making a mental note to ask Alice Morely to pack a chest with books. They had not noticed that the daylight was fading until they stepped into the small windowed room. Rosalie went back to the window in the parlour. The trees in the distance glowed pink and gold.

''Tis time we were gone,' Michael said, leading her by the hand back into the hall. 'I'd not intended to be riding with you after dark.'

Rosalie laughed. 'Then your intentions have greatly changed, Mr Pendeen,' she said. 'There's been many occasions that I've ridden with you after dark.'

Michael opened the stiff, heavy door, locking it behind them.

'When we're wed,' he said, 'you'll have no need to ride home after dark, 'twill...' He broke off, hearing hoofbeats approaching. 'Who the devil?' he exclaimed, straining his eyes in the twilight as he heard a horse whinny and saw a figure at the gate.

'Tom!' he breathed, frowning.

Rosalie stood in silence, waiting. When Tom reached them, she saw worry on his face.

'We've a visitor, Michael!' he called, glancing at Rosalie as if he wished her elsewhere. ''Tis one of the lads you've been seeking.'

Rosalie let out a startled gasp. 'Peter? Ben?' she cried.

Tom shrugged his shoulders. 'I've no notion which one. 'Tis one of them. Jack rode with him from Padstow. The lad's all in. He'll be right enough with food and rest. Mother's put him to bed with some broth.'

Michael did not speak. He ran to the gate, cleared it in one leap; then they heard hoofbeats fading fast. He had always dreaded that ill would come to Rosalie's brothers. She was always so confident they would return safely. His dearest wish since she had come back, was to bring the boys to her, and watch the joy on her face. Was he to be consoling her now? He kneed his mount faster.

When Tom and Rosalie rushed breathlessly into the living-room at the farm, Michael was coming down the stairs. His face was tense, but he looked Rosalie straight in the eye and flashed her a quick reassuring smile.

''Tis Peter,' he said. 'He's well enough.'

Her heart slowed its racing, but when she spoke her voice was hardly heard. 'Ben?' she whispered.

Michael put out a hand. She took it and felt his firm grasp.

'He's alive, but in France. Come and see

Peter.'

She followed him up the stairs, still gripping his hand. When she stepped into Michael's room and saw the figure on the bed she stood motionless and stared. Was that Peter? Could the thin, pale figure be her rosy-cheeked, mischievous brother? He turned his head and saw her. Tears ran freely down his bony cheeks and his lips said her name. She ran to the bed, falling on the floor beside him. She laid her own cheek beside his, her face already wet with her own flooding tears.

'Peter!' she whispered. 'Oh, Peter.'

Michael sat on the bed, knowing the question that would come next.

'Peter tells me,' he said cautiously, 'the *Padstow Mermaid* was taken when they went into French waters for repairs. The crew were imprisoned, but Peter escaped before they took him. He found a ship back to Cornwall. I'll take my boat on the next tide. We'll try to get him out.' He avoided saying Ben's name. He avoided saying the terrible words: Ben is in prison.

Get him out. He saw Rosalie's face change as the words reached her already shocked brain. He had never thought to remind her of those terrible hours she had spent in Bodmin Gaol. Her eyes filled with terror as she remembered her own despair and humiliation.

'I'll come with you, Michael,' she said. She saw Mary Pendeen in the doorway. 'Will you care for my brother whilst I'm gone?' she asked.

'There's no cause for asking, m'dear. You know 'twill be done.'

'You'll not come, Rosalie.' Michael's voice came to her now. Stern; determined.

'But I must, Michael. Ben may need me.'

'Peter needs you here. I'll tend to Ben.'

She searched frantically for reasons, excuses. 'I speak French. I can translate for you.'

She saw a slight twist on Michael's lips; he was hiding a smile. '*Tu est tres belle, Mais—tu ne-voyager pas avec moi sur la mer.*'

Rosalie pulled herself to her feet and stood looking down at him. 'You speak French!' she exclaimed with surprise.

He laughed. 'D'you think I've been trading on French soil all these years without learning a little of the language?' he said.

'But you will take me with you?' she pleaded.

He pulled her down on to his knee. 'I'll not take you with me, however you ask.'

They heard Mary Pendeen going down the stairs. Only Peter remained; lying warm, safe, and unafraid at last. He stared with astonishment as Rosalie put her arms around Michael's neck and kissed him. Whatever would Robert say, he thought. But then, what was Rosalie doing in Cornwall anyway? He'd thought she'd be married to Robert by now. That was partly why he and Ben had run away, so she didn't have to worry about them any more. And here she was, kissing this strange man. He seemed a decent enough fellow, but not in Rosalie's class. Still, he sighed and closed his weary eyes, he had said he would sail to fetch Ben. That was all that mattered for the moment.

CHAPTER SIXTEEN

The *Rosalie* trembled all over as she thudded down into a deep trough; to be tossed up again on the next gigantic wave. Michael had seen the storm coming. The mild westerly breeze had veered north-west and blown itself into a gale through the night. He had not sailed on the next tide as he had wished. It would have been foolish to take the boat out past the Doom Bar with such a wind blowing in the darkness.

Sailing down the Cornish coast had been wearying work. The wind hard against the starboard beam had forced them to trim the sails continually to avoid being thrown on to the treacherous rocks. The ill-lit and unbuoyed coast, which gave so many bounteous wrecks to the Cornish people, was no stranger to Michael. Yet he was always glad to be away from her sunken reefs and perilous currents.

Once around the Lizard, through the Scillies

and well into the English Channel, they ran before the wind with full canvas set. George crouched at the helm, his whole weight bent on keeping the tiller firm, the wind dead astern, the swell high.

Michael glanced up at the heavy sky, low clouds racing above them. The boat, the clouds, all blown along by the same cold blast. He swung under the forward yard, taking an angry kick at a pile of nets and oilskins in the bows. The bloody weather *would* change. Today of all days, when he'd problems enough. He straightened suddenly; looked down at his feet. No—no—no. 'Twas not possible. As his foot gained the deck, he willed it his imagination. He'd felt movement in those nets, something recoiling away from his foot. He bent double quickly, took a firm hold of one side of the nets, jerking it upwards. Rosalie rolled out on to the deck.

Michael did not speak. He made no exclamation of surprise. He just closed his eyes, hoping that when he opened them again she would be gone, that his eyes were playing tricks to please his heart.

When he opened them, she was still there. She tried to sit up, but said nothing. She saw anger in Michael's face, the kind of anger she had seen when he had fought with the man on Trebarwith beach. He turned over a fish-box, half-dragged and half-carried her on to it, then pulled the nets off her legs.

'How the devil d'you get ahead of me?' he breathed with surprising harshness.

Rosalie bit her lip, staring down at the floor. 'I rode behind you—all the way,' she said, her voice scarcely heard above the wind.

Michael folded the nets away; then leaned on the gunwale.

'I'd a notion I heard hoofbeats. I stopped several times.' He still spoke sharply, the lines on his face set hard.

'Yes—I know. I hid when you stopped.' She looked dolefully down at the deck again.

Michael nodded his head slowly. 'Aye, 'tis clear now. You came aboard when I went for George.'

The boat took a dive, shuddered, then came up again with her decks listing heavily to port. She took in water. Michael vanished from Rosalie's sight in a flash. He and Jack struggled to get the mizzen sail down before the boat capsized. The lugger heeled over to starboard; most of the bilge water swilled out as she came up again and steadied. Rosalie clung to the foresail mast. She was drenched to the skin, but still in the boat. She could hear Michael shouting. The canvas that stretched above her started to fall. When it folded on the yard, George leaned over it, shouting to her. She wondered what Michael had told him.

'The Capt'n says you'm to go astern.' He began securing the sail, then, seeing her frowning, baffled expression, he shouted again. 'The back.' He waved his arm, indicating direction. She stumbled aft, clinging to anything that came within reach as the lugger continued to roll.

Michael had taken the tiller. She sat down on the other side of it. She could see two more men now. Jack, whom she knew, was raising the mizzen canvas again. A small, thin man was helping him. Michael was silent, leaning on the tiller as George had done. His face was still dark with anger, made worse by the fact that he had not shaved, the black shadow of a beard plainly evident. His anger was partly for himself now. Why had he not told her, made it clear why she must not come? The last person on earth he wanted on his boat when he sailed into French waters today was Rosalie.

The wind seemed to be backing, the seas not so high. The sun flashed for a brief second, then vanished again.

He allowed himself to take a glance at her face. A sad, disillusioned face. The fine features, the delicate skin, the soft hair. Why had she forgotten the bloody revolution that was raging in France? About the guillotine? And she distantly related to the Duke of Rutland, at that. Anyone could see she was not in the same class as he.

He sighed. Was he too prejudiced? He did, after all, think her the most beautiful woman in the world. But if only he had told her why she must not come. He glanced again at the girl by his side. This time he met her gaze, held it. His anger was softened.

Rosalie found courage in his eyes. 'Why is it so terrible, what I have done, Michael?' she asked. 'I know the sea is rough, but I am not afraid, not with you here.'

He looked up at the sky with exasperation and groaned.

'But I am not God, Rosalie. I can't protect you from everything.'

He closed his eyes for a moment, seeking words to explain.

'The greatest fear—I've for Ben—'tis that he'll be foolish enough to boast of aristocratic blood—that he'll tell them he owns a mill—lives in a great house. There'll be war with France soon enough, Rosalie. There's no love for the English on French soil now. An English gentleman's son'd be prize enough for the guillotine.' He did not look at her face. He knew how it was. He went on, 'So—now—I've the English gentleman's daughter to worry on, too.'

He sighed, pulling her arm across the tiller so that he could hold her hand under his. 'Well!' he said resignedly. 'We'll make the best of it. You're none too clean from your hiding.' He smelt the fragrance of perfume and smiled. 'You still smell like a lady. You'd best wipe your hands in the fish-boxes, smooth them over your face and hair. 'Twill make you smell better, and put some oil on your face.'

Rosalie cringed at the thought, but she made no objection. It was her own doing. She must take the consequences. She smeared herself as he had said.

'Can you make plaits of your hair? Tie them round your head.' Michael frowned; such a foolish thing to be doing, trying to make a beautiful girl as unattractive as possible.

He was pleased with the results. Rosalie's efforts to plait her own hair, something she had never done before, were none too successful. The untidiness of the plaits, made worse by the wind and spray, was effective. There was a blackness that came from the wet wood of the boxes. He was pleased there was no glass for her to see her face.

George came over. He studied Rosalie, grunted, and nodded his approval. 'We'd best tell a like tale, Michael,' he said.

'Aye.' Michael nodded, looking up at the sky. The clouds were breaking up. A patch of blue had appeared to the south. A short distance away from it, streaks of yellow radiated from a glowing hole in the deep grey.

Michael lashed the tiller whilst he talked. 'Ben,' he began, 'is my dead sister's son. He's a wild imagination. Lest he's been telling too much of the truth. Rosalie, his sister.' He looked straight at George. 'You and the others had best call her Rosalie, whilst we're here.' He conceded this regretfully. He had hoped they would be calling her Mistress Pendeen when next they met.

Rosalie tapped Michael's arm. 'That makes you my uncle,' she said worriedly.

'Aye, it does. So mind it.' He lifted a warning finger. 'And if I'm slow with my French, I want no help from you. Yours is likely too good.'

George shifted his right foot from off a lobster basket. He put the other one in its place. 'We'd best be knowing the lad's father's name,' he suggested hopefully, 'an' his mother's for that.'

Michael looked at Rosalie expectantly. He could not remember her mentioning his father's name, although she had talked of him often.

'Edward, Edward Harvey. My mother's name was Emma, but Ben never knew her.'

'Emma! Oh!' Michael's mouth gave a slight twist of humour. 'A fair name—for a sister.'

Rosalie scowled; but inside she glowed a little warmer to see his anger waning.

The drop in the wind had eased the lugger's rolling considerably. Michael had the foresail hoisted again, and they crossed to the French coast well before sunset. Michael said little. He sat at the tiller, his eyes fixed ahead, his thoughts deep. Rosalie did not disturb him. She knew he was making plans. She saw now that he did not need her on this voyage. She had thought to be of help, to be part of the planning. She was hindrance to him, just another responsibility when he had enough already. She wished miserably she had not come.

A mile off Roscoff, Michael brought the lugger to anchor.

'We'll sail in openly,' he said when the crew came astern for their instructions.

'Straight in 'arbour in daylight?' Jack was dismayed, shocked.

George fingered his beard thoughtfully, but said nothing.

The small man called Moses stared at Michael for a second, then exploded. 'That be bloody suicide, Capt'n. *Padstow Mermaid* sailed i' daylight, i' good faith. Look 'ee what 'appened to 'ee.' He turned away, then back again quickly. 'We'm no 'gittimate papers, no bloody more'n 'ee.'

'Hold your tongue, Moses!' Michael shouted angrily. 'I'll have no swearing on my boat with a lady aboard.'

Moses scowled, mumbling under his breath. 'Not right, i' wasna', bringin' a wench, an' callin' she a lady at that. Men wasna' men who couldna' speak their minds.'

Michael ignored his grumbling and went on, 'We'll put in whilst 'tis still daylight. I've a letter here for a Frenchman I know. I did him a small service once.' He grinned, just slightly. 'I fished him out of the Channel when his boat capsized; landed him on French soil. He owes me a favour—I'll go ashore alone. George'll keep the lugger out to sea.' He glanced involuntarily at Rosalie. He had to convince her to do as he said this time. 'If—if I don't return, George'll sail for home. You'll try another way to get the lad.'

'Michael! I will not go back to England and leave you here.'

The startled declaration from Rosalie was no more than he expected. He did not look at her or make any comment. He nodded to George, who took the men forward to get the boat underway.

'Michael!'

He took her face in his hands, kissed her; then he unlashed the tiller and headed the lugger towards Roscoff.

'You wish to help me, to make things easier for me?' he said as they sailed.

'But of course I—' Rosalie began.

'Then you'll do exactly as I say,' he interrupted almost curtly. 'On this boat, I'm the captain. I'll not have you interfere with my orders. I've known George most of my life. I trust him completely. I want you to do the same. If George says you sail, then you sail. If I've to worry about you, then my mind'll not be on the task I take.'

He searched her face. He saw doubts in her eyes, then indignation, then the sense of what he said overwhelmed her and she nodded dumbly.

Michael sighed; relief, then sadness. Parting again, and so soon. No certainty even that he would return. They could all be thrown in prison. The friend he had made—the French magistrate—he could be away from home; even dead, for all Michael knew. He might've forgot his promise to return the favour. Michael had faced the threat of imprisonment, or death, many times. Freedom, life itself, were so uncertain to him that he took each day for itself. This day, this bright day in June, he wanted his freedom as never before. To see Cornish soil again. And the house he'd bought. And Ben, the lad he'd never seen, for whom he was taking such risks, he might be dead of gaol fever or ... He stopped thinking and concentrated on taking the lugger in.

'We're in sight of the coast with a glass, Rosalie,' he warned. 'Take heed. I'm your uncle. You'll not be too concerned when I leave.'

Minutes—fathoms of French water went by. Then George took Michael's place and they came alongside the quay. There were several French cutters visible. The *Padstow Mermaid*, under military guard, and minus her sails, was anchored near by.

Two armed Frenchmen appeared on the quay. Michael spoke to them in halting Breton French.

'I have a letter for Monsieur Jacques Lefevre of Santa Paul. I am called Michael Pendeen. Enquire you of Monsieur Lefevre. He is my friend.'

The men looked at each other, shrugged their shoulders, then indicated to him to come ashore. He hauled himself on to the quay, catching the rope that Jack threw to him and securing it before following one of the men. The second man remained, his musket trained on the silent crew.

When fifteen minutes later the first man returned, he stood talking to his companion. Rosalie strained her ears to hear what he said. She translated to George in a whisper.

'They are free to go. The Englishman is being held whilst the letter is being sent to Monsieur Lefevre. Tell them to take their boat out in the bay and wait.'

'*Allez. Allez. Attendrez vous sur la mer.*' The man who had guarded them waved his arms out to sea. He untied the ropes, throwing them on the deck.

George put up a hand in understanding, uttering a whispered prayer of thanks. Then he took the lugger out into the Channel and brought her to anchor.

The wind blew up again during the night. It howled eerily through the masts and rigging. The *Rosalie* strained at her anchor, tossing and pitching so that her namesake slept little on her makeshift raft bed.

Dawn broke over Les Sept Iles. A pale glimmer stretched out across the island until it reached the sea. Then it burst over the water towards them.

Morning. The wind dropped again. The *Rosalie* swayed gently, waiting.

When the sun sank crimson into the western sea, they were still waiting. When George showed signs of preparing to sail, Rosalie panicked. But she discovered they were only making the short trip to Guernsey to take on the last of the *Rosalie*'s free-trade cargoes. Before midnight they were back in the bay.

Almost dawn; and Rosalie opened her eyes. The man on watch was leaning over the gunwale. She could see his black shape against the lightening grey of the sky. Then she heard voices, lowered voices speaking; she listened again, yes speaking in French.

She threw off the blankets, keeping her head down as she crept to the side of the ship. Michael was standing in a small boat with something held in his arms. She wanted to cry out with joy; she knew it must be Ben. She kept her head, kept silent, watching as her brother was passed up into the lugger; whilst Michael himself clambered aboard. Thanks and goodbyes were given to the two Frenchmen who had manned the boat, and they slipped away into obscurity.

Michael laid down his heavy burden in the warm blankets that Rosalie had just vacated. The rest of the crew had woken. George lit a lantern, hanging it on the mast. Ben's small, thin face was ashen, his eyes closed.

Michael pressed Rosalie's shoulder as a

greeting.

'He's sick, Rosalie, but there's no fever. Lie beside him and give him your warmth.'

She did as he said, putting her arm under Ben's head and holding him close.

Michael looked up at George. 'You've the kegs aboard?'

'Aye.'

'Then weigh anchor. We're for home.'

Ben scarcely moved at all as they crossed the Channel, then turned north-east. He lay still and quiet, opened his eyes only occasionally, seeing Rosalie, then sleeping again. The voyage took much longer than before. The wind gave them little help, forcing the crew to continually trim the sails to catch the variables.

They were in darkness again when Jack shook Michael's arm and grunted, 'Cutter astern.'

There was a moon tonight, but thick cloud hid it for most of the time. Michael joined George at the tiller. There in their wake just a faint shadow showed. Then a tiny glimmer of the cutter's white sails as they were caught by a short flash of moonlight. Michael swore under his breath. They were so near home. All day and night he had been held at the customs house at Roscoff. Then, at last, the message had come. He could go to the prison and take the boy.

'To get this far...' He smashed his hand down on the gunwale with anger.

'They're gaining, Michael,' George said.

'I can see,' Michael answered angrily. 'There's no time to sink 'em,' he said, meaning the kegs.

He threw himself down on the mizzen raft beside Rosalie and Ben, peering into Ben's face. 'Has he spoken yet?' he asked hurriedly.

'Y-yes.' Rosalie was startled by his urgent tone. 'He knows I'm here. What's wrong, Michael?'

'There's a revenue cutter tailing us.' He looked at Ben again. 'He'll not stand a soaking,' he said, almost to himself. Suddenly he began untying the raft. When it was free, he lashed Ben to it. Rosalie stared.

'Michael!' she cried, in utter confusion.

'Jack, take the helm,' he shouted, dragging the raft across the deck.

Rosalie followed him, terrified; with no understanding of what he was doing. George joined them. Michael grabbed him by the shoulder.

'We're near Trenance. Take them to Matthew,' he said, starting to lift the raft on to the gunwale. 'Drop anchor, Moses!' he shouted.

George was already lowering the foresail.

Michael pulled Rosalie to him. 'You're to go with George,' he said hoarsely, 'to my brother Matthew's. 'Tis not far. Whatever happens, you're to go straight there.'

She opened her mouth to protest, but he

closed his arms tighter round her and kissed her. 'Don't make it harder, my love. Do as I say.'

George was back. They began lowering the raft into the water. George hung over the side, dropping on to it just in time as the sea parted it from the boat. Michael picked up Rosalie, waited until the raft swung close again, then lowered her down carefully to George.

'Lie down flat!' he called. 'Hold fast to the ropes. The current'll carry you to the beach.'

She lost sight of him then. The raft started moving away from the lugger. She saw the white sail go up again. It seemed to move faster, floating away. She gripped the ropes, lying on her stomach, and prayed. The raft climbed the waves and fell with a thud, but it stayed well afloat. George was silent. Rosalie lifted her head a little and saw the revenue cutter passing the spot they had just left. The raft dived; she lost sight of the cutter.

Suddenly, there was a loud thunderous boom. She tried to sit up and was almost thrown off the raft. The moon appeared again, slowly shedding unwanted light. Another boom. A flash of red. Then they saw the *Rosalie* in the distance, her foremast plunging down into the sea. The raft hit the bottom, grounded on the beach, safe. The revenue cutter fired again at her now moonlit target. The *Rosalie* shuddered, splintering, crashing; then she split in two.

A cold hand gripped Rosalie's heart as she watched. She had involuntarily climbed off the raft and walked back into the surging sea, as if she could reach out to save the boat that bore her name. In her mind, she saw the beach at Trebarwith on the night of the wreck, the sea choked with wreckage from the East Indiaman. She saw the dead sailor whose body had drifted on to the beach. No one had cared. But Michael had cared; only Michael. Would he, too, be washed on some cold, unwelcoming sands? She started walking blindly into the sea. She felt strong hands on her shoulders, pulling her back. She heard George's voice a long, long way away.

He dragged her back on to the damp sand, keeping a firm hold on her.

'We'd best get the lad inside,' he said, untying Ben with his one free hand.

Ben? Ben! She had forgotten Ben. Was God so cruel he had given her back her brother and taken Michael in his place? She looked back at the sea.

'We must get a boat,' she whispered. 'Michael.'

'... Matthew,' George said. 'I'll bring Matthew.'

She followed him numbly as he carried Ben up the beach. It seemed too far, much too far from the sea. Yet Matthew's small farm was only a short distance away.

When the door was pulled open, Rosalie

collapsed at the feet of Matthew Pendeen.

CHAPTER SEVENTEEN

Lowing cows; seagulls; footsteps on slate; the cowshed door slamming. Sounds Rosalie had become accustomed to whilst staying at the farm. Then she opened her eyes, suddenly startled. This was not her room at the farm. The curtains, the furniture were different. She heard steady breathing beside her on the bed and turned her head quickly. There lay Ben, still painfully thin, but a little colour returned to his cheeks. Her movement woke him; he opened his eyes and smiled.

'Are you better, Rosalie? I'm so glad. I was so afraid. Oh, Rosalie, I'm so sorry.'

Sorry? About what was he sorry? Oh, running away. She took his hand in hers, squeezed it, and kissed his cheek. Then she stopped, quite still. Something was wrong. Something she could not remember. She heard footsteps coming up the stairs. A strange woman came into the room and smiled at her.

'I'm Peggy,' the woman said, 'Matthew's wife.'

Matthew?—Matthew! The eldest of the four Pendeen brothers. Memory flooded back. Rosalie sat bolt upright, her hands clutching at the bedclothes.

'Michael!' she cried. 'Where's Michael?'

Peggy Pendeen leaned forward, putting a comforting hand on Rosalie's shoulder.

'We've nay found 'ee yet, m'dear,' she said quietly.

Rosalie stared. What did she mean? They had not found him yet. Had they not taken a boat to rescue him? The words tumbled out, accusing, distraught, anguished words.

Peggy heard voices outside and went to the window, pushing it open. Her husband was talking to a man she did not know. Then he ran inside suddenly and shouted up the stairs.

'Peggy! Peggy! Michael's alive! D'you hear? Michael's alive!'

It was the next day before Rosalie rode Matthew's horse towards Treyarnon Bay. It had been decided that it would be best for Ben if he were to be taken to join Peter at Camelford. A friend of Matthew's had agreed to ride with him, seeing him carefully into the care of Michael's mother. Rosalie was a little confused by the secrecy that surrounded Michael's whereabouts. She had been instructed to take extraordinary steps to make sure she was not followed. She had been convinced with some difficulty that she must deny all knowledge of the trip to Roscoff and the subsequent wrecking of the *Rosalie*. It was all, they told her, necessary for Michael's safety. Matthew's eldest son Jim accompanied her. He was only fourteen, but he knew the countryside well, seeming to know all the tricks of throwing off unwanted followers.

The tiny cottage they reached was tucked away in the green valley of Porthcotham. There were two rooms downstairs and two above. Jim left Rosalie at the door, saying he was going down to the beach. He would call back for her later.

Michael was sitting at the table in the living-room when she entered. He looked pale under his tan, his breathing seemed rasping, but he stood up and came towards her. She looked up at him and burst into a flood of tears.

The old woman to whose cottage Michael had been brought, got clumsily to her feet.

'Aye,' she mumbled, shaking her head. 'Aye. Lucky to be alive, the lad be. Found 'ee down on the beach, did 'ee.' She opened the kitchen door, then turned back to them. 'I be in the garden if you wants I.' She closed the door behind her.

Michael sat Rosalie down on his own chair, pulling another up beside her.

'I saw—' she began, wiping away the tears.

'I know, Matthew came last evening. He said you were ill for two days. Are you better?'

'Yes, thank you,' she smiled. 'But you—?'

He shrugged his shoulders. ''Tis nothing. When the mast was shot, I took to the water.' His face clouded, he looked down at the table. 'Jack, Moses—they did the same. I've heard naught of them.' He lifted his face to Rosalie's again. 'I was so exhausted when I reached the beach, I fell in a heap and stayed there all night. The currents were devilish strong, and against me.' He shook his head sadly. 'They were older than I. I doubt they'd make land.'

Rosalie put her hand on his. 'But you are alive, Michael. I thank God for it,' she whispered.

'Aye. Alive, and for what?' he said bitterly. ''Tis not likely you understand what is done. I need to go away, my love. I've lost my freedom. I've lost—' He broke off and did not finish. Then he sighed a long, deep sigh. 'The coastguards'll soon know 'twas my boat they sent to the bottom.'

'But how will they know? The tinners have cleared the wreckage. There's not a splinter of wood to be seen.'

'They'll make enquiries. They'll soon find the *Rosalie* missing from her mooring too long. And the tinners,' he gave a short laugh. 'They'll not be against trading her name to 'em.'

'But where will you go? For how long, Michael?'

He looked from her, then got suddenly to his feet, not wanting to answer her question. ''Tis time you were leaving,' he said. 'I hear horses. Look from the window. Is it Jim?'

She did as he said and saw his nephew waiting with the horses.

Michael took her hands in his. 'Go to Camelford; stay there, Rosalie. Tell Tom, I'll go to Chy Ryn for a while. He'll know what I mean. He'll bring you to me. Tell him to bring clothes, my books—and, most urgent, quill and paper... When I see you again—I'll likely have made plans.' He smiled. 'Matthew tells me Ben's well now. I'm greatly pleased you've your brothers back safely, my love.'

Michael seemed calm, almost too calm, for there were so many questions she wanted to ask. Yet she sensed that now was not the time.

'Chy what?' she asked.

He smiled and kissed her forehead. 'Chy Ryn. 'Tis Cornish for "secret house". Tom and I spent many hours there when we were boys. 'Twill make a good hideout for a while.' He became more serious again. 'Take care, Rosalie, trust no one but the Pendeens.' He saw her reluctance to leave.

'I'd sooner have you safe at Matthew's than here with me. 'Twill not be long before we meet again. Tell Matthew I want him to take you himself, up to Camelford.'

They parted then, and she rode back with Jim to his home at Trenance.

When, two days later, Rosalie arrived at Tom's farm, there were three letters waiting for her, all sent on by Alice Morley. The first she opened was from the schoolteacher giving her monthly report on the children at the mill. A solicitor's letter advised her that the mill had been sold, with the satisfactory result that the new owner had agreed to the terms about the school. Rosalie was pleased; at least there was something to be glad about.

The third letter, it seemed, had travelled from London to Trevia, up to Nottingham, then back to Cornwall again. Rosalie's letters were being sent under Sophie's name. The letter was from Lucy. Hugh Trevia had been killed in a riding accident in Spain; she was returning to Trevia for her period of mourning.

'I am glad that I can at least be honest with you, dear Rosalie,' she wrote. 'That I need not pretend that my husband's death is a great tragedy in my life. I have never wished him ill, but I fear I must confess I shall not miss him greatly.'

Rosalie realised that the long delay in the delivery of her letter could mean that Lucy might be at Trevia already. The following morning she put on her riding habit. She took Michael's horse which Matthew and she had brought back from Padstow as they rode through from Trenance.

Lucy was pale, although the black dress she wore looked well with her bright auburn hair.

'Rosalie! How wonderful to see you!' she exclaimed. 'The servants told me you had returned to Nottingham, yet here you are when I most hoped to see you.' She saw by Rosalie's clothes that she had ridden. 'Where are you staying? Come, tell me your news.'

Rosalie smiled a little, but shook her head. 'A week ago, I had so much to tell you, Lucy; so much to be glad of, and now it's all in pieces.'

She told Lucy of the house that Michael had bought, of her brother's return, and the need now for Michael to hide.

'He says he must go away, and, although he has not said it, I can see it in his eyes, that he means for ever, and that I may not go with him.'

Lucy frowned. 'Oh, Rosalie, if only I could help you, I would.' She was thoughtful, opening and closing her fan slowly. 'If the boat was proved to be carrying smuggled goods, and Mr Pendeen's name was on her bows, then we cannot say the charges are false. The plea that he went to France to help your brother will hold little weight in Cornwall. The magistrates are always glad of a scapegoat. They catch so few smugglers.' She sighed regretfully. 'My influence in Cornwall has been taken away from me by my husband's will.'

Rosalie stared. 'What do you mean, Lucy?' she cried.

Lucy gave a short laugh. 'My husband decided that the best way to punish me for not bearing him children, was to leave his wealth elsewhere. To be precise, to his nephew. The mine, all his shares in other companies; even Trevia and the lands and farms. I have an allowance. He did not leave me quite penniless.'

'Oh, Lucy, I'm sorry. I'd thought you would have everything.'

Lucy smiled. 'I'll not be unhappy. I shall take an apartment in London and live quietly. Our nephew has graciously allowed me to come to Trevia for six months' mourning, and to tidy up my affairs here.' She smiled. 'But this does not help you, my dear. I will have a word with the magistrate, if you wish, but if Mr Pendeen wishes to be thought dead, then it will bring to the attention of the authorities he is not. Perhaps you should ask him first.'

Rosalie nodded sadly; the world falling slowly at her feet.

Chy Ryn was a very ancient, ruined house when Tom took her there that evening after dark. It was deep in a gorge on the edge of the cliffs, completely hidden from view except from the sea. All the windows looked seawards.

Michael was much better, his chest clear and his colour returned. But he was still too quiet, still too calm. The anger she would have expected of him was not there.

'You have seen the posters in Camelford?' he asked.

Rosalie shook her head, puzzled.

'Three hundred pounds,' he said with a bitter laugh. 'That's what they offer for me. There in bold letters for all to see. Michael Pendeen, captain of the *Rosalie*, lugger. Wanted for charges of smuggling spirits without payment of duties. Reward three hundred pounds.'

'But no one will give you away, Michael. You are so well liked.'

'And well enough known to be recognised anywhere.' He took her hand. 'If you were a farm labourer earning sixpence a day, would you not be tempted by three hundred pounds?' He shook his head sadly. 'Nay, Rosalie. I'd not blame them. I've known hunger myself.'

Rosalie looked around at the bare, candlelit room. Michael had cut wood and made a raft for a bed, covering it with the straw and blankets that Tom had brought. They sat together on a fallen tree trunk that Michael had dragged in. Like the first time when they had met by the river. Michael picked up the basket she had brought.

'I've a rare hunger now. Have you brought me some food?'

He took out two pasties, went over to the fire and, laying a stone across the hob, he put the pasties to warm.

Rosalie did not feel like eating, but she ate hers when they were ready, not wanting to risk spoiling his appetite.

Black cobwebs embroidered the walls from the roof to the slate floor. Their inhabitants ran about freely. There had been cobwebs in the house Michael had bought, but this room was different; cold, unfriendly. The black squares of the uncurtained window seemed to threaten their privacy, yet Rosalie knew that outside the window the land dropped steeply to the sea, the

Atlantic Ocean, where their joyful world had fallen apart.

The candle began smoking, the flame bowed sideways, then flared up brightly before burning so low that the room was almost in blackness. Michael lit another candle from his bag, standing it beside the first one on the hearth.

''Twould be better with a lamp,' he said. 'There's so much draught.'

'I'll bring one when I come again. What else do you need, Michael?' She took another glance around the room. He seemed to need everything.

'Just the lamp,' he said, then he smiled. 'I'll likely need some more food as well.'

'What do you do all day here?'

'Read mostly. It passes the time. I mislike so much time on my hands. It goes so slow. I was reading Shakespeare today. One of his sonnets caught my eye.' He leaned over, taking out a book. 'Shall I read it? He wrote it for me.'

'Shakespeare did?'

'Aye. I've a notion he knew I'd be here like this.' He started reading. Rosalie closed her eyes, listened; understanding.

'When in disgrace with fortune and men's eyes,
I alone beweep my outcast state.
And trouble deaf heaven with my bootless cries

and look upon myself, and curse my fate.
Wishing me like to one more rich in hope.
Featur'd like him with friends possessed.
Desiring this man's art, and this man's scope,
with that I most enjoy contented least;
Yet in these thoughts myself almost despising;
haply I think on thee, and then my state
(Like to a lark at break of day arising
from sullen earth) sings hymns at heaven's gate.
For thy sweet love remember'd such wealth brings
that I scorn to change my fate with kings.'

He closed the book slowly, sighing. 'But then, perchance he was not thinking of me, for although I'll have the memory of you, I'll not have you.'

'I'll still wed you, Michael,' she said with conviction. 'We can go away to another part of the country, where you are not known.'

Michael looked up from the book, straight into her blue eyes. He got to his feet and went over to put another log on the fire. It did not need another log, but he could not be so close to Rosalie and keep his emotions enough under control. He stood with his back to her, his arm resting on the mantel-shelf.

Had she been a farm girl, or a girl from the town even, he would have made love to her weeks ago. But she was Rosalie. And Rosalie was a gentleman's daughter. Lovemaking came after marriage for her, and he had been willing to wait. But could he wait now? Wait for ever? But, then, she wasn't his to take, even if she were willing. And he was sure she would be... But what if he gave her a child, then went away and left her? What sort of man would he be then?

'Michael?' Her voice broke the torment of his thoughts. He turned slowly to look at her, the decision taken from him by the mere fact that he loved her so much.

'I'll never wed you, Rosalie,' he said slowly, 'not whilst my name's so tarred. If I were took, 'twould mean transportation to Australia—if I escaped the rope. Matthew and Tom came last evening. They're finding a ship for me—one sailing for America. I'll stay at sea for a long time—go ashore only on foreign soil. I'll not mind being so much at sea, Rosalie.' He leaned his head on his hands for a moment as if he found it difficult to go on, then he stood up straighter; turned back to face her. 'I'll mind not having you. You're the sunlight in my life—I was a fool to think it ever possible; perchance 'tis better this way.' He came back and sat down beside her.

'I'm concerned at what you'll do now.' He took a paper from inside his coat and held it out to her. She opened it without speaking, and read:

Dear Mistress Harvey,
I beg leave to acquaint you that I was successful in perchasing the property known as Lowarth Tek for you as requested. The price being the sum you suggested. The title deeds await your signiture at the offices of Trenwith and Son, Solicitors, Bodmin.
Your obedient servant,
Michael Pendeen.

Rosalie stared dumbly at the letter.
Michael's voice broke her confused thoughts.
'Another trick of fate, Rosalie. I bought the house in your name, for the reasons I told you when we were there. Now, it seems, 'twas most wise of me. There'll be no problem for you to have the house.'
'Michael! This is ridiculous!' she cried. 'The house is yours. The money was yours. We will get it sold again. I will bring you the money.'
He smiled at her. 'What'll I do with so much money at sea, my love? I bought the house for you. 'Tis yours to do as you will. I'd prefer that you sold it and went back to...' He broke off. Where would she go back to? Her home was being sold. Her brothers were in Cornwall. 'Back to Robert,' he said firmly. 'There's more money hid at the farm. Mother'll tell you where.'
'Lucy will see the magistrate if you wish it, Michael.' The words burst from her lips.

'Lucy! Lady Trevia! She's here?'
'Yes, Hugh is dead. I told her—'
'You told her where I was?'

'Michael!' She was shocked, firstly that he should think her so stupid, then that he did not trust her friend.

'She must go to no magistrate. 'Twould make no difference, anyhow. I'm dead. I drowned when my boat was sunk.'

Footsteps, then a long, low whistle pierced the night outside.

'Tom's back for you.' He held out his hands and pulled her to her feet. 'Forgive me, my love, for promising so much and leaving you with so little. To have known you as I have, to have you love me—these are memories I'll always cherish. We'll meet again before I sail.' He stroked her hair, feeling its softness. 'When I lie in my hammock, I'll close my eyes and dream I'm walking in the garden with you. You in a blue silk gown, and I—' he smiled, 'dressed as a gentleman should be dressed, with white breeches, a white silk shirt, aye, and a scarlet muslin cravat. Then I'll laugh, that I should ever have thought me worthy to be your husband.' He kissed her. 'Go now, Tom's waiting. Take care, and mind you close the door behind you.'

She turned to him, smiling, as she left. For there was no door, only an open doorway to the cooling night.

CHAPTER EIGHTEEN

Peter Harvey reined his horse quickly and swore with all the vehemence of a weathered sailor. The bridle path was completely blocked by a fallen elm. He took the mare back, patted her neck affectionately, then rode her clear over the tree with little difficulty. Another flash of lightning lit the November night sky, forking down to earth over Bodmin Moor. The horse shied and stood trembling as the thunder rumbled nearer. Peter leaned forward, speaking gently into her ear.

'Go on, girl; go on, Shadow.'

She went on, trotting through the deep mire.

The rain, driven hard against them, made Peter bend low on the mare's back. He wore breeches that were too large for him, tied with string at the waist; a grey wool jacket with fraying cuffs. His cap, too, was over large, which had the effect of making him look even younger than his seventeen years. He rode without a saddle. When the next flash startled the already nervous horse, he almost lost his seat, heaving himself up just in time and kneeing the horse on.

Suddenly, the rain came faster. The lightning streaked its way in quick successive flashes. The rolls of loud thunder became indistinguishable one from another. The mare halted abruptly, throwing her head in the air as she whinnied with terror. Peter slid helplessly down her neck into the thick mud. When he got to his feet he swore again, not at the frightened horse but at the sky that was making his journey so intolerable.

He caught the mare, tightened her head rein, and began walking, leading her beside him, talking to her as he might a nervous child. The lightning cracked on the path ahead of him. The sky flashed red, then blue. Had he been indoors he would have marvelled at the sight, but here on the road he wished it was black, plain black, and quiet.

When, half an hour later, he saw the still, gentle glow of a lantern, he sighed with relief.

'We're home, Shadow,' he said, stroking the mare's soft nose.

A dark figure came running towards them.

''Tis you, Master Peter. The Lord be praised. The mistress be that worried about 'ee.' He put up his arm to take the horse.

'See she's well dry, Mansel. It's been a rough night.'

'Aye, Master Peter, that I will, that I will.'

Peter opened the door to find Rosalie running down the stairs.

'Oh, Peter! Peter! I thought I heard a horse. Was everything...?' She broke off and smiled. 'No, don't tell me now. Go and change first. We'll make you some supper.'

He climbed the stairs gladly, emerging

twenty minutes later looking like the young gentleman that he was. His fair, still wet hair was tied back in a blue bow, his well-fitting, dark-blue breeches set off by his white cotton hose.

Rosalie was in the parlour, sitting close to the glowing coal fire. She patted the chair beside her. Peter sat down, holding out his hands towards the welcome warmth.

'Where's Ben?' he asked suddenly.

Rosalie smiled. 'He's a slight cold. Alice sent him to bed early. He wasn't too pleased.'

Peter laughed. 'There was no Alice to send us to bed early when we were at sea. We fell in our blankets with gladness at the first opportunity.'

Rosalie's face paled a little, as it always did when she was reminded of Michael, exiled, it seemed, to a life at sea. He had sailed from Plymouth on the First of July, riding there under cover of darkness with Tom by his side.

Rosalie had been bitter when he had gone. Bitter against society, against the law. She had not considered her own loss so great; although never a day passed when she did not long to hear his voice, to see his dark, laughing eyes. She had been angry mostly that he had lost everything he had worked for.

'She's cost me many nights' rest, and years of hard work,' he had said of the *Rosalie* when he had shown her off at Padstow. All those years' work. All the planning. All for nothing but what he could have had if he had never tried. A job as a mate on an American-bound packet schooner. Bitterness had made Rosalie defiant. She would not allow his work to be for nothing.

She had kept the house he had bought, employed the servants he had wanted, sent for Alice Morley as he had told her, and she had continued to run the smuggling ring herself. It had not been easy; knowing whom she could trust and whom she could not was the hardest. She had started with George. She knew that apart from the Pendeens he was the only one who knew that Michael had been his own master. She had, with difficulty, persuaded George to take over the purchasing and arranging of cargoes with the agents in Guernsey. George was the only man who came to the house and saw Rosalie. Always by night, by the back door. George gave instructions and payment to the captains of the boats they contracted to run the goods. Tom, riding into the towns as he did anyway on farm business, did the bargaining with the merchants. Rosalie's brother, disguised as Peter had been tonight, rode with instructions to the men who unloaded and delivered the cargoes. The boys had both developed the ability to use a Cornish dialect, and quickly acquired a knowledge of the countryside.

The parlour door opened. Alice Morley came in with a tray of hot soup and toasted muffins for Peter. She had been delighted when Rosalie had asked her to come to Cornwall, but not so pleased when she had learnt what her mistress intended doing. Faithful always to the Harvey family, she had sighed resignedly, concluding that she would not be successful in an attempt to dissuade Rosalie. She had stayed, knowing that at least she could make sure they were well fed and clothed; even if they did ride out into the night on such harebrained schemes.

Rosalie had been sad that she could not visit Michael's mother openly as she wished. It had been decided that public contact might bring suspicion on either family. She rode to the Pendeens' farm under cover of darkness for an occasional chat with the woman whose daughter she had hoped to be.

Peter finished the soup and muffins and started on the coffee that Alice had just brought.

'Tomorrow night is all arranged, Rosalie,' he said; only now finding the breath to enlarge on his wet ride. 'John Redenek has fifteen men to ride. That should be enough. With the cargo being mostly tobacco, they'll not need so many horses, either.'

'Did you remember to ask him to get someone to check the safety of the mine?'

'Yes, he agreed it was a good idea. He said some of the riders still worked the bal. He's getting them to go down and take a good look.'

Rosalie sighed with satisfaction; another cargo planned without problems. They were really doing rather well. She was able to pay the men good money, too, which pleased her because she knew it was what Michael had done. But what would Michael say if he knew what she was doing? He would disapprove, of course, considering she was putting herself in too much danger. She tried hard not to think what her father would have said. He might have given her a little credit for being a good business woman, but doing something so against the law, and involving his sons—

She put the thoughts to the back of her mind hurriedly. When boats they contracted were sunk by bad weather or their crew captured by the customs officials, Rosalie had at first felt acutely guilty; but as the months had gone by she had become hardened to it. As Peter had said, if the boats were not working for her they would be doing so for someone else. And she did pay them better.

The following day, Rosalie wrote her fortieth letter in her attempt to secure a pardon for Michael. Most of her letters were returned, having been seen by very junior clerks. Others received a curt reply requesting proof of innocence. Proof of innocence was the one thing that could not be got. Lucy Trevia, before she had returned to London, had ascertained that kegs of gin had been picked up by the revenue boat when the *Rosalie* had been wrecked. A tinner had sold the wood from the bows with Michael's name on for five guineas. Proof of his guilt was overwhelming. That Michael had only been on his boat because he had gone to rescue Ben was of no importance. The three hundred pounds for information leading to his capture was still standing. The magistrates she had visited had laughed in her face.

The fortieth letter was returned with the usual curt note. It was Ben's thirteenth birthday, a day when the family would be celebrating and a small party held at Lowarth Tek. The persistent rain of the last two weeks had stopped at last. After a handsome tea, Rosalie and her brothers went into the garden, the boys for a game of croquet, Rosalie just to walk. They had wanted her to play with them, but she was not in the mood for their jokes and teasing.

Mansel Polruan had indeed done wonders with the garden, as Michael had said he would. The masses of flowers that had bloomed through the warm summer were wizened and gone by now, but there was still colour to be seen. The holly berries, bright in clusters on their shiny leaves. The ivy, ringing the tree trunks with its pale yellowish-green blossoms. The moss carpet shone emerald green after the wet. Rosalie put her hand on to the hawthorn and broke off a twig. Its red berries still wet from the rain. She tossed it idly into the air, watching it fall on the other side of the gate.

Tom Pendeen caught the hawthorn twig, wondering why it was flying through the air at him.

'Thank you,' he laughed, seeing Rosalie and realising she had thrown it.

It was unusual for Tom to visit in daylight. He had decided that one visit to a neighbour could not be construed as conspiracy.

'We'd a letter from Michael,' he said, still not sure whether he was doing right to tell her.

Rosalie's face told him she wanted to know.

'He's well, liking the ship he's on. Bound for South America next, he says.'

Rosalie listened, her heart thumping. Was there no message for her? Had not Tom brought the letter to read? She saw no letter. There was no message. She had always hoped that Michael would write to her, yet she had known he would not. He had been so resigned to his fate, so sure that it would be best for her if she left Cornwall, that he would do nothing to give her false hope. She did not blame him. Perhaps it was easier for him to forget if all contact was broken. He did not know she lived in his house.

Tom came in for some birthday tea; assured them that his mother and Sophie were well. And gave them the happy news that Jenny, his wife since the harvest, was expecting a child in midsummer. He had imparted the news with a mixture of pride and embarrassment. After congratulating Tom, Rosalie went to her room and burst into tears. Suddenly, she was jealous of Jenny Pendeen. Jealous because Jenny was carrying the child of the man she loved and she, Rosalie, could not.

During the next few days Rosalie became increasingly restless. She was more and more disillusioned that she was unable to do anything at all towards getting Michael's freedom. If only she knew someone in the High Court, someone with influence. Her family had been well known in business circles, but had no connections with Parliament. Her claim to be related to the Duke of Rutland was genuine enough, but the distant in it was very distant and hardly an asset. It had been Robert's family who had the titled connections and friends who were Members of Parliament.

Robert! ... Rosalie sat still just where she was, looking out of the window in Ben's bedroom. Why did she not seek Robert's help?

CHAPTER NINETEEN

Emily James took a sip from the small china coffee cup, leaned back on to the wide comfortable chair and sighed with satisfaction. She had just persuaded Robert to give a Christmas Ball this year. The sense of achievement she felt was quite justified. Robert did not like giving balls at any time. She drank the remainder of her coffee, got to her feet and pulled the bell cord. When the servant appeared she asked for a quill and paper, then sat down at her writing desk. Robert was so moody these days. He never used to be so. Quite inconsiderate all this rushing off to London for weeks on end. Well, anyway, he was back now. She intended to see that he stayed here. Making arrangements for the ball would keep him occupied.

The door opened and Baines stood there.

'Your pardon, Ma'am, but Mistress Harvey to see you.'

Emily James sat motionless. 'Mistress Rosalie Harvey?' she enquired, her eyes staring, wild with dismay.

'Yes, Ma'am. She asked for Mr James, but I told her he wasn't in, Ma'am.'

Robert's mother pulled herself together hurriedly, turning her head away from the waiting butler.

'Show her in, Baines,' she said as coolly as possible, knowing the old man's affection for Rosalie.

Rosalie stepped nervously into the pale green drawing-room and waited for the hard, critical words. The prospect of facing Robert again had been daunting enough, but to have him out and his mother receive her was ten times worse. She would as soon face an armed coastguard as Robert's mother.

Emily James turned from the writing desk, studying her guest. Then she smiled. A fixed, squeezed-up smile, but she smiled.

'How nice to see you, dear,' she said as patronisingly as possible. 'Are you up from Cornwall on holiday, dear? Do sit down. Will you take coffee?' She rang the bell again.

Rosalie swallowed hard. 'I—I wished to see Robert,' she said nervously.

'Yes, dear. Baines told me. Such a pity he's still away. But then, I do not suppose you travelled all the way from Cornwall to see my son.' The last words were emphasised to underline that she alone possessed Robert.

'Away!' Rosalie stared at her hostess's still smiling face.

'Yes, dear. He is in London. We do not expect him back for some time.' She glanced involuntarily out of the window. At least, she hoped he would not be back for some time. He had said he was going riding. Or was it shooting? Anyway, either meant an hour or so, and he had only just left.

A knock on the door heralded a maid with coffee cup for Rosalie and the quill and paper.

Emily James sat down and poured coffee for her guest. 'How are you all, my dear? I understand your brothers returned safely after all.' She made it sound like a crime.

Rosalie had written a brief letter to Robert informing him that Peter and Ben were safe and that they were all remaining in Cornwall.

She had not mentioned Michael.

'We are all well, thank you. Alice Morley is still with me, as you no doubt know.'

'You have not—? No, you could not have done. I—er—rather thought you had plans to marry in Cornwall.'

'No. I have not married.'

'You—er—lost most of your money when the mill was sold, I understand, You are—er—' She was not allowed to finish.

'Oh, no. We still have a remarkably good income. The boys' inheritance is quite untouched, of course.'

Cannot be here for the money, then. Robert would be fool enough to give her some if she did ask. He was still very touchy about her name, in spite of the way she had treated him.

Rosalie had finished her coffee. She began to rise.

'Yes, of course, dear. I must not keep you. No doubt you are staying with friends. Well, I will tell Robert you called. Though, heaven knows when I shall see him again.'

She sent up a quick prayer of forgiveness for that one.

Baines was summoned. He showed Rosalie out.

'If I may make so bold, Mistress Harvey,' he said, 'the master'll be real disappointed to have missed you.'

'Thank you, Baines.' She turned and climbed into the waiting carriage. When they were outside the main gates, she told the driver to stop. She paid him, then climbed down and watched him drive away. She could not be so near without taking a look at her old home. Just a glimpse. She started walking towards Rayleigh Wood. Finding Robert in London might not be too easy, but at least she could stay with Lucy.

Her boots snapped the dry twigs as she walked. She walked slowly, remembering. A cock pheasant strutted on to the path, jumping into flight when he saw her movement. The earth was dry underfoot, but there was still the damp smell that always hangs about woods in winter. She heard several woodpigeons cooing, one to another. Then a shot rang out; a small brown object fell dead at her feet. She saw it was a woodpigeon and stepped to the side. Rustling amongst the bushes told her that its murderer was coming to claim his prize.

'Rosalie!' Robert saw her long before he could be seen. He walked towards her slowly, blinking, hardly believing his eyes.

Rosalie stared at him as if he were the last person on earth she would have expected to find shooting in his wood.

'Your mother—your mother, said you were in London,' she stammered.

'Did she, by gad? Well, I'm not. I've been back for over a week.'

Rosalie flushed. She had prepared herself to meet him, and now here she was so surprised that she was tongue tied.

Robert picked up the woodpigeon, putting it in his satchel. 'If you'll come back to the house, I'll have something to say to Mother,' he said angrily. 'You did come to see me?' he asked, suddenly realising he might be assuming wrongly.

'Yes—I wanted to talk to you.' She looked down at the earth, wishing she was anywhere but here. When she looked up again he was staring at her ungloved left hand. She knew with embarrassment he was looking for a wedding ring.

'Where are you staying?' he asked hurriedly, reddening slightly.

'At the Coach and Horses.'

'Then you must come to Rayleigh,' he said. 'You can't stay at a place like that.'

'No, Robert.' Rosalie was quite definite. 'I can't face your mother again. It would be better not. Can we talk somewhere—somewhere else?'

His eyes searched her face; saw she meant it, then he sighed.

'We could go to the old summer-house,' he suggested. 'It will be a bit dusty, but then—' He was about to say, 'We never minded that in the past'. Suddenly, the past seemed a long, long time ago.

'That would do well, Robert.'

He picked up the gun that he had leaned on an oak, and they walked back through the wood. The door to the summer-house creaked, almost falling off its hinges when Robert forced the door open. There were no children here now to use it as a ship, a school or whatever took their fancy; Robert picked up a cane chair, shook it thoroughly and tried to blow off the dust.

Rosalie sat down on it and crossed her fingers.

Robert laid his gun on the wooden table, edged himself beside it and waited.

'Well, Rosalie,' he said at last, seeing she was reluctant to begin. 'To what do I owe this—unexpected—and pleasant surprise?'

'I came to ask you a favour, Robert,' she said.

He smiled. 'I rather thought you did. Is it money you need?'

'Oh, no, Robert! I have plenty of money,' she cried.

Robert raised his eyebrows. She had had little enough left after sale. He had expected that one day she might come to him for money. He would always have given her some, made her an allowance as he had said he would in London.

'I—I would like you to use your influence to get a free pardon for someone who is charged with smuggling.'

Robert laughed, suddenly relieved. 'I should not think that too difficult,' he said.

'Would you really do it?' she cried eagerly.

Robert was suddenly disturbed by the look of profound joy that came into her eyes. He had thought of a servant. Rosalie had always been a fool about her servants. He remembered when her groom had got drunk and had been arrested for brawling in the street. She had paid his fine and written a letter to the magistrate. But a servant would not be so important to her as this.

'What sort of fellow is this—this smuggler?' he asked.

'Well, he—' Rosalie flushed. How could she describe Michael? She took a deep breath and went on. 'It was he who found the boys for me. You remember I said someone had found the ship they were on. Then—when Ben was in prison in France—'

Robert's eyebrows nearly touched his hair.

'He took his boat and went to rescue him—at great risk to himself. The boat brought spirits back from Guernsey on the way. A revenue cutter attacked it; the ship was sunk. Being the owner of the boat, he is now a wanted man and cannot set foot in England, so you see—'

'But if the boat was sunk, what about Ben? This man?'

'Oh—he put Ben on a raft with one of his men, then swam ashore himself.' She had decided not to mention that she was on the boat.

Robert sighed with relief. He could see now

why Rosalie was so grateful. It was the boys. He looked down at her, sitting in the cane chair. Suddenly, she belonged there, sitting where she had so often sat before. He decided there and then that he would not let her go this time. He still wanted her, more than ever before.

'I'll make you a bargain,' he said, jumping down from the table, standing in front of her flushed and excited. 'I'll get a pardon for this man—if you will marry me.'

He had really meant it as a joke, a way of broaching a subject that was difficult now for him to broach. He saw shock in Rosalie's eyes, almost fear. He saw her desperately struggling with the problem as though she had to make a terrible decision.

'I meant it as a joke, Rosalie, the bargain part, that is. But I still want to marry you. Don't leave me again, Rosalie. I—' His voice was pleading, begging.

Rosalie covered her face with her hands. She could not look at him.

Robert stood quite still where he was, his fingers drumming on the table. The noise seemed loud in the long silence between them.

Rosalie spoke at last, pulling her hands slowly down her face. 'I cannot marry you, Robert; for I love someone else.'

Robert's fingers stopped drumming; he leaned back on the table as if needing support.

'This man? This smuggler?' he said quietly.

'Yes.'

'And you expect me to get him his freedom so he can marry you?'

Rosalie did not answer.

Robert's voice became loud, angry. 'Well, I will not do it, Rosalie. I will not plead for some—lawbreaking peasant who has the impudence to want you for his wife.'

'And if I married you, Robert? Would you do it then?'

Robert's breathing stopped visibly. Not a muscle of his body moved. His anger melted into doubt, as he feared he had not heard right.

Rosalie had suddenly seen things more clearly. She had seen that for Michael his freedom was most important. He would have the house; the smuggling ring still, if he wanted it. Most of all, he would have a respectable name. That was important to Michael. It would be little price for her to pay really. If the boys had not run away, if she had never met Michael, then she would have married Robert without a doubt in her mind. She would put back the clock. Michael would find some Cornish girl to share his life. He had never been wanting in girls to take to a fair or a barn dance before he met her. She had always known that.

Robert was relaxing, seeing sunlight ahead. 'Do you really mean what you said, Rosalie?' he asked, his voice breaking with emotion.

She nodded slowly. 'I'll give you his name, and the details,' she said calmly. 'I shall return to Cornwall. On the day that you give Michael Pendeen the papers that confirm his pardon, you may announce our betrothal. I'll marry you a month from that day.'

CHAPTER TWENTY

A treacherous cross-wind gusted southwards across Padstow bay on the 14th June. The pale grey mist that it carried blanketed the coast, hiding the Gulland Rock Island intermittently as if playing hide-and-seek, taunting any ships that dared to venture towards the bay.

As the timber-laden schooner *Canadian Maple* neared the coast, Stepper Point loomed suddenly out of the mist; then vanished. The tall ship entered the narrow channel, snaking its way under the point. She passed the lifeboat station at Hawk's Point, then turned sharply eastwards. She ignored the churning sea that bid her drop anchor till the mist had cleared. Her navigator knew full well that to hove-to here would mean a dragging anchor when the tide turned. Confused, swirling seas that meant certain death as the ship foundered helplessly on the rocks of Gun Point, or the sands of the bar. Skirting safely round, the schooner headed southwards again. She sailed smoothly through the shoaling water, until at last she came to rest beside the busy quays of Padstow

Harbour. Sheltered there from the wind and free of mist, her Canadian captain sighed thankfully, their safe passing of the perilous Doom Bar due entirely, he knew, to the wisdom and experience of their first mate.

A tall, lithe figure sprang from her decks well before she was moored. He ran hurriedly down to the North Quay, his face as anxious as if the weight of the world was on his young shoulders. Apprehensively, he glanced around him, avoiding the eyes of anyone he passed. Soon, he turned into the front parlour of the George and Dragon. He scrutinised its midday occupants carefully. He had come to meet someone, whom he did not know.

A man stepped towards him, hesitated, then smiled.

'I think we have met once before, Mr Pendeen,' he said.

Michael Pendeen stared; his heart went cold, his mouth dry. Standing in front of him, the smile still on his lips, was Robert James. Was it a trick? The letter that had bid him set foot on English soil for the first time in almost twelve months. Was it a forgery? Had Robert James enticed him there to have him arrested, transported to Australia for life? He did not know.

Robert James gave a short laugh. 'You are surprised?' he said.

'I am amazed, sir. Are you having play with me?'

'Indeed I am not. Come—I wish to talk with you. We have the back parlour to ourselves.'

Michael followed, still wary; still half-expecting the customs men to appear and the scant freedom he had to be gone in a single, unguarded second. He sat down at the table, silent and pensive. He thanked the landlord for the ale that was placed in front of him, watching suspiciously as Robert James paid for it and dismissed the man.

'Your pardon, Mr Pendeen, is quite genuine. You are quite free. There is no longer a price on your head.'

The worried lines that furrowed Michael's brow became a little less intense. He drank his ale slowly, but still did not speak. His dark eyes looked steadily at the elegantly dressed man across the table from him.

Robert put down his own tankard and took papers from inside his coat. He handed them to Michael without comment.

As Michael read, a faint hope began to dawn for him, a longed-for hope at the end of a year-long existence of hiding, of staying at sea; avoiding even friends he knew, trusting no one. The Judge's letter seemed genuine enough. He smiled a little, the ease with which he had laughed a year ago now foreign to him, the joys he had known part of a distant past.

Robert tapped the table impatiently with the silver head of his cane.

'You are convinced?' he asked.

Michael nodded. 'I am convinced, sir, and I thank you, if 'tis to you I owe my freedom.'

Could he ask after Rosalie? How much did his companion know?

Robert nodded thoughtfully. He lifted his tankard to drink, yet before it reached his lips he changed his mind suddenly; banged it down on the table, spilling his ale.

'Confound it, sir,' he cried. 'I wish to ask you some questions. They will seem impertinent,' he warned, 'but I beg you to be truthful.'

Michael took a clay pipe from his pocket, filled it with tobacco, then lit it with a taper from the fire, a habit he had learned from his Canadian captain. He could guess what was coming.

'I'll answer your questions,' he said at last, 'and truthfully.'

'I understand,' Robert began, 'that Rosalie and you, sir, were—more to each other—' he hesitated, seeking suitable words, 'than one might have expected.'

Michael grew tense, his mistrust returning. 'You are asking me, sir,' he said, 'to confess to a close relationship with your wife, before you wed her.'

Robert smiled, shook his head, then laughed. 'Rosalie is not my wife, Mr Pendeen.' He did not add, 'yet'.

'She has not wed?'

'No.'

'Then I'll tell you that we'd hoped to be wed.

I'd bought a house. Then Ben was imprisoned and—' He broke off. 'I suspect you know the rest.'

Robert nodded. 'Tell me,' he said. 'Do you still wish to marry her?'

Michael looked him straight in the eye. There was a humour in Robert's eye that he did not much care for. 'My possessions, Mr James,' he said, pointing to his bag. 'Those things you see, hardly the possessions of the future husband for such a lady. What I'd wish, and what I may do, these are—well...' He did not finish. He emptied his pipe in the grate, finding no pleasure in it now.

Robert finished his ale. Then, as he spoke, a wry smile crept over his face. 'Peradventure, Mr Pendeen, there are more surprises in store for you. I suggest you take a walk back along the quay. I doubt in your haste you noticed the cutter moored there. If you care to look at her bows, you will find your own name. Mistress Harvey has not been idle in your absence.'

Michael stared. He saw undisguised amusement still in Robert's eyes; yet it could hardly be a joke. He got to his feet and crossed quickly to the door.

His step was visibly lighter as he set off down the quay. He passed the *Canadian Maple* without a glance, staring in disbelief at the ship behind her. A cutter certainly, but that proved nothing. He jumped a pile of lobster baskets easily; skirted round a group of fishwives without even seeing them.

He gazed at the cutter's bows. *Kingfisher*, a name he might have chosen himself. And there, in bold black letters, was his own name. Robert James had spoken the truth. Michael sat back on his haunches, admiring her. A beautiful ship, the ship of his dreams. She had seen rough weather already, but he knew she had ridden it well.

He stood up slowly, looking along the quay, wishing for the first time for so long to see someone he knew; to show them his ship, to spread the news that he was back in Cornwall, a free man.

As he looked, his body grew suddenly tense, every muscle locked, his pulse began racing. Along the quay, dressed in a pink muslin gown, her fair hair blown by the breeze, was Rosalie. She was pacing backwards and forwards as if waiting for someone. Was she waiting for him? Had Robert James sent him here, knowing he would meet her?

He glanced down at his clothes, suddenly aware of his own shabbiness. Would she recognise him? It was only a year, but he felt so much older. His hand went to his chin, to the thick black beard that grew there. He wished he had had time to shave it off. She had never seen him with a beard.

He started walking, slowly at first, then faster. He could not wait for fresh clothes, nor a shave. He had to know now.

Rosalie stared down at the ground as she walked. She was annoyed with Robert's insistence that she come to Padstow with him. He knew it held too many memories for her, yet he had been adamant that she come. She sighed. Well, she would have to get used to doing what Robert wanted soon enough. She had not been surprised when he had come down to Cornwall. It was, after all, natural that he should want to see her. He had spent a good deal of time in London during the last months. She knew he had obtained the pardon for Michael. But the bargain had two parts. He had to give it to Michael; and finding Michael was seeming impossible. She had been waiting for Robert half an hour already. What business he had in Padstow she had no idea. She gave a deep sigh of exasperation, and looked along the quay for him.

The eyes that met hers were not Robert's brown ones, but black, like the thick curled hair and the beard. And the eyes shone as they gazed down into hers. She cried his name with joy; his lips found hers and her heart was lifted to the skies.

Months of longing, of praying for this moment only increased the happiness she felt. Then, abruptly, the sky fell, shattered into small pieces on the grey cobblestones. She tried to turn her face away from him, but he kept on kissing her, oblivious to the lead band that was gripping her heart. She pushed hard against his chest. He laughed; then he saw the sadness in her eyes.

'What's amiss?' he whispered.

'Your ship,' she said, pointing to the cutter. 'That's your ship.'

He traced his fingers gently around her face. 'I know,' he said. 'Robert told me. He gave me the papers of my freedom. I owe him a great deal.'

'Yes, you owe him a great deal.' She repeated the words automatically, bitterly.

'I owe you even more, my love, but there'll be time enough to thank you.'

'There will be no time, Michael.' Her voice was strange. He stared at her with confusion.

'Rosalie,' he said demandingly, 'what's troubling you? Pray tell me this instant.'

'It is—Robert,' she stammered, desperately searching for courage.

Michael stared at her. His arms slackened their grip. 'You mean—you are in love with him now. You wish to wed him?' he asked, keeping his voice steady with difficulty.

Rosalie did not answer. She searched frantically for the right words. Should she tell him the truth? Would it be better to let him believe otherwise?

A voice beside her saved her the trouble. 'Rosalie has promised to marry me, Mr Pendeen.'

Michael's arm dropped from her waist. He looked first at Robert James, a satisfied grin covering his face, then back at Rosalie, her eyes as full of misery as the day he had left her.

'You wish to wed Mr James?' he asked doubtfully.

She nodded, avoiding his searching eyes.

Robert James walked a little away from them.

'A word with you, Mr Pendeen,' he said.

Michael went towards him with more than a little reluctance.

'I have been making extensive enquiries about you, Mr Pendeen,' Robert said, the amused grin vanished at last. 'It would seem you are well thought of in these parts.'

Michael hardly heard what he said. He was watching Rosalie. Something did not make sense. Something was wrong. If he had to lose her again, he would do it with grace, but only if it was what she wanted. He noticed suddenly a slim, red-haired figure in a brilliant green gown walking towards them. She stopped beside Rosalie and tapped her arm.

'You are going too far, Robert,' she scolded, regarding him with frowning eyes.

Rosalie stared. 'Lucy!' she cried. 'What are you doing here? I thought you were still in London.'

Lucy smiled. Robert came over to her. She slipped her arm through his.

'I fear I have been misleading you, Rosalie,' he said. 'You see, when I was in London, acquiring a pardon for Mr Pendeen, I saw a good deal of Lucy. When she found out about—' he glanced at Michael a little uncomfortably, 'our bargain, she was shocked. And I—er—saw her point. Well, to be brief, Lucy and I discovered we enjoyed each other's company so much that she has done me the honour of agreeing to be my wife. So, you see, I cannot possibly marry both of you.'

Rosalie's eyes shone with absolute joy. She flung her arms around Robert and kissed him.

Michael closed his eyes and sighed, understanding at last.

Robert laughed. 'You see, Mr Pendeen,' he said, almost with embarrassment, 'life is full of surprises. In all the years I have wished Rosalie to kiss me like that, she only does it when I tell her I cannot marry her.' He patted Lucy's arm affectionately, then took out his pocket watch. 'By gad!' he exclaimed. 'We're late for our luncheon engagement at the George.'

He went towards Michael, putting out his hand. 'Goodbye, Mr Pendeen. Take good care of her. And be warned, she is headstrong and wilful.' He laughed. 'But, then, I think you know this already.'

Michael nodded, smiling. 'Aye. I know it well.' He came back to Rosalie and took her hand.

They stood silently together, watching as Robert and Lucy walked arm in arm along the quay. As they turned the corner, Robert raised his hat and bowed good humouredly to two

Padstow women on their way home. The younger one put her hand on her mother's arm.

'Did 'ee see, Mother? That gentleman took his hat off to we.'

Her mother smiled. 'Aye, a wealthy one, too.' She stopped walking and stared across the harbour. 'Why, Emma!' she cried. 'Be that not your cousin Michael yonder?'

Emma followed her mother's gaze with surprise. 'Aye, 'tis 'ee,' she cried excitedly. 'Let's go to 'ee.'

Her mother held her arm. 'Nay,' she said. 'He's talking to a lady.'

Emma watched, disappointed. Then she scowled as the tall figure bent his head to kiss the lady in his arms.

Mistress Tregar stood shaking her head. 'D'you not see who 'tis?'

Emma did not see.

''Tis Rosalie,' her mother said.

'The mill girl he brought!' Emma exclaimed.

'Aye, the mill girl he brought wi' hands so smooth an' soft they'd not done a day's work in their lives.' She sighed. 'We've work to do, my girl. He'll visit we soon enough. An' I'll wager when 'ee do, he'll be dressed like a gentleman.' She smiled and shook her head. 'But then, your cousin Michael always was a gentleman.'

We hope you have enjoyed this Large Print book. Other Chivers Press or G. K. Hall Large Print books are available at your library or directly from the publishers. For more information about current and forthcoming titles, please call or write, without obligation, to:

Chivers Press Limited
Windsor Bridge Road
Bath BA2 3AX
England
Tel. (01225) 335336

OR

G. K. Hall
P.O. Box 159
Thorndike, Maine 04986
USA
Tel. (800) 223–6121 (U.S. & Canada)
In Maine call collect: (207) 948–2962

All our Large Print titles are designed for easy reading, and all our books are made to last.